STILLIFE

Titles by Herb Haslam

Fiction
Stillife, Selected Writings
Going Back For Jeremy, A Novel
Wintercrossing, Selected Stories
Ribbons of Light, Stories and Poems
for Children/Young Adults

To be released in 2004
Fiction
The Metaphormers
Shadow Realities

Non-Fiction
Incyte: Melody of the Mind
Spheryx, A Graphic Exploration into Work Flows

For further information about these
and other publications visit
www.windspur.com

STILLIFE

Herb Haslam

WINDSPUR PRESS

www.windspur.com

– An Internet-Focused Company –

Published by
Windspur Press
http:/www.windspur.com
An Internet-Focused Company

Cover and Interior Design by Val Sherer,
        Personalized Publishing Services
Cover Art by CGX Design

Manufactured in the United States of America

ISBN 0-9724915-3-8
Library of Congress Control Number: 2003098463

To that very special group of artists, counselors, staff support, UN Delegates, students and friends who gathered together on the shores of the Atlantic Ocean one memorable summer to demonstrate that when we are primarily connected by our collective imagination, however briefly, life on this earth knows no boundaries.

CONTENTS

NURTURING INTELLIGENCE

Mr. Schoonmaker, would you come to my office, please?"

Mid-afternoon in a public school, not the best moment for an exploratory chat. Principal Harold Poke straightened up papers on his desktop while he waited. Soon, with a knock on the door, the rumpled form of Schoonmaker leaned his head in.

"Yes, sir?"

"Come in, Randall, sit down."

"I have a…"

"This won't take long. I was passing the teacher's lounge a while ago and I couldn't help noticing that what appeared to be a disagreement was taking place, a discourse carried on with a good bit of shouting which we simply don't permit, and I couldn't help notice that you seemed to be playing a rather prominent role in the shouting. Would you care to enlighten me, Mr. Schoonmaker?"

"Well sir, it's…complicated."

"Try me."

"It's…it's…"

"Schoonmaker, what the hell was the big argument about?"

"Education, sir."

"What about it?"

"Well, we were discussing, when it comes down to it, what its purpose is and what its purpose should be. Sir."

"They're not the same?"

"Some of us don't think so, sir. Some of us…"

"You, in particular."

"Myself in particular do not feel, does not feel comfortable with the present system."

"How so?"

"It needs improving."

"Well, good Lord, young man, everything needs improving. Do you have something a little more specific in mind, perhaps?"

"Our argument is about what we are supposed to be doing. We know what we are hired to do. We know what tests and standards are to be met. We know what content is required. We know that it is our burden to push and pull certain students on each year, to catch certain students falling by the wayside each year, to keep the classrooms as orderly as possible so that learning has a chance to take place and to be familiar with as many family situations as possible each year."

"You know these things?"

"We do."

"Then what…?"

"It's like there's too much of a load to get into a little cart. In the end, the horse can't pull it at all."

"Clarity?"

"In the end, our graduating students are not getting jobs. You know that, we all know that. This throws the question back on us...what should we be doing about it?"

"I see."

"It's not a pretty picture and it is getting worse."

"Really. Schoonmaker, how is it that you know the employment picture so well? Have you been talking with anyone about this outside of the school?"

"Some."

"Some?"

"A few."

"A few who?"

"Well..."

"Come on, Randall, be a little more forthcoming, if you don't mind."

"Sure, well, I've talked with some of the employers in the community. Some of the supermarkets managers, restaurant managers, auto repair shop owners, the CEO of a petroleum compressor plant, you know, like that."

"And what did they say?"

"They said that if we were a business, we would be closed by Friday. They said there is work out there but the kids can't handle it. They said that they do not want much—a clean driver's license, free from drugs, good work habits, a good attitude, even better if they were problem solvers— and as we have them for thirteen of their eighteen years, we should be able to deliver that much."

"We are not our brother's keeper, Schoonmaker."

"Sir?"

"We are not required to track each student, you know that, don't you?"

"Sir."

"If we had to track each student when he or she leaves here, it would require putting on fifteen more office staff, do you realize that?"

"Some said that we have a marketing problem."

"A what?"

"A marketing problem—our product is backing up, we cannot market our product in the economy."

"What the hell are you talking about?"

"Unless and until we introduce a little quality control into our system, as far as some are concerned, the system is superfluous."

"Superfluous?"

"Some say the level of intelligence is so low as to be negligible in our departing graduates' classes. Some say they will never get a job on God's green earth with this kind of poverty stricken training we call education!"

"I DON'T GIVE A RAT'S ASS WHAT ANYBODY OUT THERE...yes, Ms. Kellerman?"

"The shouting?"

"The what?"

"The shouting, we were all getting kind of worried out here in the office about the shouting."

"No one's shouting, Ms. Kellerman, we were discussing a serious matter, you can go back to work now, thank you. And close the door, thank you. Mr. Schoonmaker, don't you think I am aware of what's going on? Don't you think I have my sleepless nights about what's going to happen to our kids down the road? But at the same time, I have had to let eight people go this year. Four of them were teachers. The budget was slashed again. No band, no art classes. Classes doubled up. Too many kids in one room. Security is first priority. We do not have an acceptable level of security in this building, Schoonmaker. The building has problems, plumbing, heating, windows, paint, the playground needs repairing, Schoonmaker, money for instructional supplies has been cut back, Randall, as you well know, the kids do not have books and resources to get an adequate grounding in many of the subjects, never mind computers, lowest on the list, Schoonmaker, AM I MAKING MYSELF CLEAR, HERE, SCHOONMAKER? WHILE YOU ARE RUNNING AROUND INVESTIGATING POSSIBLE FEELINGS OF DISSATISFACTION OUT IN THE COMMUNITY AT LARGE, RANDALL? It's all right, Mrs. Wilson, we're al-most finished here, look, tell Ms. Kellerman and the oth-ers to take a little break right about now, ok? Thank you. Close the door, thank you. Would you like my job, Randall?"

"No, sir."

"What would you do if you were in my shoes, Randall, I want to hear it from your lips. Speak."

"I would try to explain to those in authority that we have gotten off the track with the best intentions. We are not able to do what we are charged with having to do."

"Which is?"

"Prepare young people for a productive place in society."

"It is May 10, Randall. What would you do, say, May 11?"

"I would announce that unlike previous summers, the school will be closed for three months until September."

"Whom would you announce this to?"

"All stakeholders—and that means everyone. The business community, the Board, City Hall, the parents, the teachers…the school would be closed for rebuilding. Everyone will be needed. Planning would start the first of June. There are repairs to be made, supplies to be donated, labor to be provided, but most of all, the purpose of the school must find a new definition. It can no longer afford to be disconnected from business, industry, government, the community in general, it must take its rightful place again, side by side with all the rest who try to help make this place a working neighborhood. We are after nurturing intelligence, Mr. Poke!"

"Nurturing what?"

"Nurturing Intelligence, that's what we need to be about. And the mark of an intelligent person is that he knows, she is aware, they participate, solve problems, they care."

"Hmm."

"After all, school is about knowledge. Knowledge acquired over several years. And we live in a world impacted by information every minute of every hour. But no one understands that in school. No one understands that there has been a revolution in technology caused by instruments of information—computers. We are trying to run a training institution and the student body, by and large, does not know the implications of the word digital!"

"What do you propose, Schoonmaker?"

"That all the computer manufacturers be given a chance at providing software and hardware to our school, a pilot school committed to nurturing intelligence. And with the help of everyone we can get interested, students and adults alike, something mighty fine will come out of this effort, benefiting each and every individual, and we will have a school and a student body and faculty and an administrative corps that understands and cares about one thing and one thing only..."

"Nurturing intelligence."

"Right!"

"Are you finished?"

"Yes, sir. Finished and leaving right now, Mr. Poke."

"Do you want to do this thing?"

"Oh yes, more than anything."

"Can you devote the summer to it?"

"Yes, I can."

"Then I suggest you get to work immediately and draw up those announcements, the responsibility is yours. Be ready to get underway by June 1."

"YES, SIR!"
"And Randall?"
"Sir?"
"Count me in."
"Yes, SIR."
"One more thing."
"Sir?"
"Make that Harold."

MIMI

Seven years had slipped by since he first had met Mimi. She had a sway to her walk and a seductive play around her eyes that had caught his attention immediately. But she was married and, athough he was separated, when he learned of her two young children, he tried to keep his admiration of her at better than arm's length.

But the connection was there, nevertheless, and over the years whenever he had occasion to cross her path—at the technical services center where she worked, at holiday get-togethers for clients, associates and staff, or just passing on the street in that small city, the look said it all.

For him, with love in his marriage at first seeping then simply draining away like an ebb tide, this communication between him and Mimi slowly built into a conscious urge to undress her, caress her, make love to her. As for Mimi, normally fastidious in manners and behavior, having lived with the fact of this invisible link, she had long since enjoyed sharing a good laugh or winks in a crowded meeting room, discreetly leaning against his shoulder now and then as her way of acknowledging the familiarity that had grown comfortably between them.

He felt her acknowledgement most strongly on the phone. With no visible action to be covert about, he came to tease her, when the party he was calling was not available, by keeping her on the line in the midst of activities and other personnel hovering nearby, discussing increasingly personal aspects of her life, her needs, and finally her desires.

Mimi had married young, born two children in quick succession, and then returned to her professional life at the same time her husband had been promoted to regional responsibilities that kept him away for several weeks at a time. Richard maintained it was an investment in their future, that the next rung up would mean no longer having to travel, that she should try to be patient just a little while longer.

But Mimi was lonely. Over the years, being a warm and sensual woman, she had distracted herself with the children, with her job—she had risen to managing the large seismic processing lab—and with her few close female friends. But little by little she found herself warming to the idea of a relationship that could be closer at hand, one where she could renew a vibrancy she felt had slipped away from her over the years.

And Carl was very attractive. He was a quiet person, a geophysicist now working more and more with seismic technologies. His close-cropped graying hair gave him a look of seriousness that his conversations belied. She found herself responding to his attention, encouraging his suggestiveness, making herself available to him as he passed through the offices and work rooms in short, intimate moments when they were out of observation.

Lying in bed alone after the children had quieted down, she let herself imagine what it would be like with Carl, where it might take place, under what circumstances it might happen, normally, naturally, excitingly. She knew there could be little defense against what he might whisper in her ear in an empty office hallway now and then, thinking about what lay beyond the whisper.

"Oh, you noticed!" she found herself blushing into the phone one day when he had called to speak with one of the technicians who would not be on the premises for the rest of the morning, asking then for Mimi's extension.

"Yes, you look really great again in that black pants suit you haven't worn for awhile."

"Haven't been able to wear for a while," she corrected. "You're very sweet to notice."

"What's going on over there, anyway, Mimi? Everybody out today?"

"Might as well be. They're all working on the new round of project contracts coming up. Why, are you planning to come by?"

"Want company, huh? No, I don't think so, too many around for me to do what I would really like to do if I came by."

"Carl, what are you talking about, whoa, I'm about to be surrounded, but don't hang up, talk to me so I can answer yes or no, the others won't notice anything then."

"Well, let's see, what are we talking about here? Something warm?" He chuckled at her predicament.

"Yes."

"Something tender?"

"Oh, yes."

"Am I on the right track?"

"Oh, yes. More."

"More what? More closeness?"

"Yes."

"More intimacy? More feeling?"

"Yes."

"Are you still surrounded by others?"

"Yes, go on."

"Well, would you consider doing something with each other regarding what we have been talking about?"

"Yes." Mimi paused and then added in a low intense whisper, "Yes."

It was a conversation with a life of its own. It had taken the lead and both of them were following along obediently. Carl was so aroused by now that he was on his feet by the drawing board in his office unable to sit quietly any longer.

Mimi wedged herself up against the corner of one of the graphics display tables, pressing against it as inconspicuously as possible.

"Shall I go on?"

"Go on, please," Mimi murmured into the phone, smiling and nodding at one of her staff who was holding a black and white survey proof up for her approval.

"Hands," Carl went on, "would you like to feel my hands…"

"Yes."

"…slip around you, undress you, are you wearing a blouse?"

"Yes."

"Shall I unbutton your blouse, then undo your belt, slip your skirt down so that you could step out of it?"

"Yes, please." She motioned to another staff person that what they wanted was in one of the bins of tubes holding large transparencies.

"Are you standing there now with just your bra and panties on?"

"Yes, I am, I could be."

"Do you want me to stand behind you and gently pull you in?"

"Yes, yes," she nodded, smiling to an associate, "go on."

"Are you ready for me to undo your bra now and help you slip it off and pull your panties down or do you want me to undress first?"

"Either way," she lowered her voice, "either…way…" She was a little breathless. Then trying to recover, "You can ship tomorrow, or for that matter today."

"Would you like to take off my clothes yourself?"

"Yes."

"My jacket, my shirt, my pants, my shoes and socks…"

"Carl," Mimi whispered in a husky voice, "I can't take this any longer, let's just do it, ok?"

"Now?"

"Yes, here, now, how soon can you get here?"

"Ten minutes."

"Meet me at the other building, then park in the alley. I'll let you in the warehouse door. Hurry!"

"I'm on my way!"

Carl raced to the elevator bank, rode down holding his jacket in front of him so that his arousal wouldn't send young clerks and secretaries squealing in all directions, and drove to the alley entrance as fast as the midafternoon downtown traffic would permit.

Mimi was there, waiting, and held the door open while he paused, drank her in, then slipped through.

"I only have about twenty minutes before they will wonder where I am, so let's hurry," Mimi breathed in the dark into his ear. "Follow me," she added, quickly leading the way to the entrance of the supply storage room. They entered and she locked the door behind them.

"I took the only key," she said. Inside the large room the only light came from a small skylight at the other end. There was nothing but shelving full of cartons of every size in row after row. Toward the back there was a long table used for opening and documenting incoming materials.

She leaned back against the table turning toward him and they kissed hungrily, soft at first, their mouths soon opened and tongues, on fire with anticipation, fought to dive deepest into each other's throat. Bodies trembling, their clothing fell to the floor and in a moment they were on the table wrestling nude with little yelps of excitement and exertion.

And then the storm had passed—it was over. Mimi slowly stopped her lifting movement, the aftershocks subsiding little by little until she was lying quite still. Carl felt like he was floating in outer space with a perfect loving companion, carefree, his mind empty, spilling over with feelings for this wonderful woman and the intimacy she had given him.

"I hope I didn't tear your pants," Mimi giggled, as they began to separate themselves, "trying to get them off so fast. Better check, just in case." She pushed and pulled her clothing back into place.

Carl found his shorts, his pants, his shirt, his shoes, his jacket, found the strength to put them all back on, adjust everything, and began to walk toward the door with her through row after row of storage cartons. But he was still in an aftermath of incomparable lovemaking. What next? Where would it go from here? He had to see her again, soon.

Mimi used the light from the open warehouse door to check her looks in her pocket mirror, fluff her soft curly blonde hair, and add a dab of lipstick. She felt heroic. Her desire had quieted down. She was in command again. She loved what had happened. She was complete. She pulled the big door farther open so Carl could slip out.

"See you," she said softly, shutting the door behind him and locking it, planning to return by the most expedient route through the inside of the connected buildings.

It all happened so fast, Carl was still trying to—what? Make plans? Say goodbye? What?

"I…" was all he got out as he heard her retreating footsteps on the other side of the closed door.

He drove slowly back to his office.

There were several phone messages.

An associate asked if he wanted to take a coffee break. "Later," he said, looking out at the afternoon, the outline of rooftops, some smoke, a cloud, birds flying past in the distance.

Seven years.

His mind was still trying to fit what had happened into some kind of manageable place. There was no place. But the feelings, "What about my feelings," he asked himself. "Mimi, I love you, why didn't we do this the night we met?" And he heard himself answer, "Because we were and are both married, there are children involved, our own homes, our own private lives, responsibilities, the look of things, social codes... doesn't matter," he thought, "I needed her, I've always needed her."

He reached for the phone to see if she had gotten back to the top floor of her office building and if things were in hand and if she was all right... "Mimi?"

He could not possibly know that Mimi had just gotten off a long distance call with her husband who had told her that the pending transfer had come through, that he had arranged reservations for her to fly out and meet him that weekend, a short day away, in the city where they would be moving, several hundred miles distant, that their new life was about to begin, that everything looked great and that he wanted her to see a house located by his company, he had even taken time to track down a place he could come home to every night, a place for them to move into as soon as possible.

"Hi, Carl."

"Are you ok?"

"Uh huh."

"It…I…"

"I've got to go now."

"I love you, Mimi."

Silence. Carl heard the voices of staff personnel in the background. But something else in her tone…he could not know…but he strongly sensed.

"I must talk with you."

"Can't work, it wasn't wrong, it was wonderful. But it can't work."

"Can I see you tomorrow?"

"I'm going away tomorrow."

"But…"

"Goodbye, Carl." And the phone clicked in his ear.

He knew. He didn't want to think anything and at the same time he knew. He would never forget the sound of such terrible finality. He shuddered as he felt abandonment for the first time sweep through his being. That strange and wonderful tether that had connected them so unquestionably for seven years had just been let go at the other end, dissolving his orientation, letting him drift out weightless into an endless night sky by himself, completely alone.

LABYRINTH

A fellow by the name of Lester Hawkins came through these parts not long ago looking for someone I had not seen or heard from in several years. He said he owed this man some money, quite a bit of money, and he wanted to pay it just to get it off his conscience. He asked if I knew this guy and I said yes, at one time, I certainly did. Then I asked him how he figured into those times. He said that between knowing most of the players and being in and out of several deals himself, he had been able to piece together most of it. He looked at his watch, asked if I had eaten yet. I hadn't, so we walked to the only decent place in town, a local steakhouse, family owned and operated, which was jam-packed every noon. By now it would be easing up a bit. Once seated in a corner booth with ice tea and dinner ordered, he began.

I knew Johnny Eames from the early days when he first arrived in town as an agent for the Rocky Seismic Exploration Company out of Montana. He was a fine salesman but when that outfit went belly up during the bust at the time,

Rocky Seismic closed down its branches. This left Johnny at loose ends, not certain what to do, what with little cash, no job, and no future.

"Stranded, I think they call it."
"Right."

But you know Johnny, he did have a streak of luck of sorts and after two months of weight loss due to not eating much, a solution crossed his path as if by magic. It was about the time he met a good-looking woman called Florence at a party and they paired off right away. She was a one-time first grade teacher, widowed for awhile, lonely, and looking for a little action.

Johnny had a knack of telling people what they wanted to hear. And where potentially large profits were out there for the taking, he knew just how to paint the picture. So when Florence asked him what he did, he described what shooting a seismic line meant. He told her all about how the big vibrators are placed at points along a line on the surface of the ground and how computers catch the waves from the vibrations coming back up to the surface. He told her they could then paint a picture of what was down there that could hold oil or not. Two-dimension (2D) seismic data revealed the cross sectioning of strata; with a few more dollars 3D revealed an underworld of valleys and peaks and all kinds of interesting things from several hundred million years ago.

But Florence always got to the point right away.

"Do you want to dance, honey?" she asked Johnny.

The party didn't break up until near dawn. Florence went home to Johnny's leased two-bedroom condo for eggs and coffee. But when they got there, they headed straight for the nearest bedroom and crashed side by side.

When they woke up it was Sunday, and after a lusty round of lovemaking, Florence, who wound up on top of Johnny, her generous bosom framing his head, said, "Tell me something nice, Eamesey, honey."

Johnny looked long and hard into the future, considering the $182,000 this delectable female peering down at him claimed to have stashed away.

"Florence, if I can't make ten million in ten years, I need to get out of the oil business!" and with that, I imagine she covered his face with loving kisses and they started all over again.

First thing Monday morning, the referenced $182,000 was transferred to a business account in the name of Eames Seismic Technologies and that same afternoon, a suite of offices was leased on the fourth floor of a building mostly filled with industry-related companies.

Next thing you know, Johnny hooked up with Roy Arkin.

"You knew him, old deal makin' Big Roy?"
"Sure did."
"Figured you would."

If Big Roy didn't know everybody, he certainly knew everyone with likely money to invest and folks looking for investors. When he saw a winner in the making, he helped them out - for a reasonable piece of the action, of course.

Roy told Johnny that he could raise all the dollars he needed to get Eames Seismic on the map. And that he would do so for 49 percent interest in the company, an office, and a monthly stipend for the next five years, renewable, if things were going well by then. That sounded good to Johnny, so he agreed.

The steak platters arrived with mounds of mashed potatoes and mixed vegetables.
"More tea, gentlemen?"
"Hmm, yes, thank you, ma'am."

Anyway, it wasn't long before Roy became a partner. He set up a meeting for Johnny to sit down with a couple of board members of a local commercial bank where Florence had maintained her savings prior to its transit to Johnny's company account. On the credit strength of that money backing up Eames Seismic Technologies, a business plan was developed—a win–win business plan with opportunity for all, including, of course, the two bank board members. Among the items cited was a million-dollar revolving credit line opened in the name of Eames Seismic Technologies and, although not written down anywhere, an understanding for the two board members to receive a considerable cash reward plus a piece of the future action, specifically a five percent interest in all 2D seismic sales to be shot immediately on land already optioned for that purpose.

That night Florence and her love flew to Vegas where the next morning, Johnny made good on his part of the bargain, struck rather breathlessly in bed the previous Sunday morning, and married Florence. As this was company business, the credit line underwrote the trip and its expenses, including several thousand dollars left behind at the black jack table where Florence could easily have spent the rest of her natural life.

Now, you know that to shoot seismic, you need field crews, and to transport the field crews you need vehicles. By the middle of the following week, five new smart looking SUVs were lined up in the parking lot of the building where Eames Seismic Technologies officed, and guys came in from all over to fill out the applications.

Florence oversaw the selection and hiring of a receptionist and bookkeeper. I noticed that she favored one with thick glasses, Cissie Foster, thin, clean but certainly not a knockout, but with proven skills in what was needed for the job.

The office space filled up in no time, what with Big Roy and his secretary, a meeting room for presentations, an office for Florence to come and go as the not so silent partner, a small cubby hole for the management consultant, Gary Tate, and Johnny's corner office. The largest room was reserved for the tech lab where two heavy-duty workstations—to be managed by two geophysicists yet to be hired—would be installed to interpret the miles of film coming in from the field shoots.

So I guess all the necessary got underway in those first three months. The geophysicists were hired, the field crews shot a respectable amount of seismic in regions that had scattered or no coverage, the money was flowing nicely, and Florence was happy with her schedule. She woke at nine, had breakfast served by the housekeeper, stopped by her office in time to see what plans were made or not for lunch, shopping afterward before returning home to dinner waiting to be served by the new housekeeper. Yes, full and very satisfying days they were for Florence Eames.

Now, as I understand it, one morning Big Roy walked into Johnny's office just down the hall from his own. He sat down in front of Johnny's desk and stared across at him.

Then he asked, "Are you keeping track of those small seismic shoots you've been selling from time to time?"

"Of course, why not? What's goin' on anyway, Roy?"

"Just make sure it's all accounted for and that Cissie knows how to do it right, ok? My friends from the bank which gave you a million-dollar credit line will be wanting their commission one of these days, that's what's goin' on."

"Don't worry about it, it will all be taken care of, you'll see. Besides, what are they going to do, complain to a judge if they don't get paid off?" Johnny had to chuckle at the thought.

"Don't be shortsighted, Johnny," Roy said, holding in his real explosiveness about Johnny's attitude, "this is how the game is played. If you sit down at the table and try to ignore the rules, the house will pick you up, wring you dry and toss you over the horizon. So don't screw around, honor your obligations, that's all."

Johnny was annoyed at the idea that those two guys could force him to do anything because, after all, they were illegally representing their own interests. He was not going to give them a cent unless and until he was damn good and ready. But Big Roy said he was not going to raise the matter again; he would assume Johnny was doing the right thing.

For Roy, it was a question of not wanting the matter sitting on his desk—not so much the principle.

Johnny's roving eye was limited to legal blindness levels between Big Roy's strict observance about paying attention to business and business only, and Florence, who insisted that Johnny wear his cell phone on his person every hour of the day. Johnny spent most of his office time on the phone or in meetings. He was open to any and all possibilities, never the shrewdest, he was never short of action.

About two weeks later, after Johnny failed to answer messages left by the bank directors, both board members showed up at his office door. Roy ushered them in and they shook hands all around and sat down.

"More tea, fellows?"

"You know, I think I'll switch to coffee."

"One coffee coming up. Two?"

Lester nodded.

Johnny leaned back in his big chair and said, "Now, what can I do for you fellows?"

"Well, we were concerned about your business," one began.

"Concerned? How so?" Johnny smiled his most winning smile.

"Concerned because you are not answering our calls, concerned because several months have gone by, and concerned because we know you are selling the seismic you shot on speculation," the other one said.

"And we know who all you sold it to," the first added.

"I still don't understand what's on your mind this morning," Johnny said smoothly.

"What's on our mind is our five percent commission on approximately $1,640,000 sales," the second one said.

"Which comes to $82,000," the first one said.

There was a tiny nano-second beat.

"I don't see any problem here, gentlemen. Do you, Johnny?" Big Roy interceded in his benevolent dictatorial way and shot Johnny a warning look.

Johnny leaned over the intercom.

"Cissie, are you there?"

"Yes, I am."

"Good. Would you cut a check for…?"

"Sterling Enterprises, Inc.," both directors said together.

"For Sterling Enterprises, Inc. for $82,000 and bring it into my office?"

"Of course, Mr. Eames, sir."

"I've got another meeting, running late, good to see you boys," Roy said, and the meeting was at an end.

Attention to detail combined with good judgment was all Johnny needed to worry about for this was a potential turning point in the good affairs of Eames Seismic Technologies.

Johnny assumed his books were in order, but Cissie was having many problems getting accurate information to do so. In short, from what she told me, it would have been almost impossible for her to produce a balance sheet at that time—never mind an accurate one. She could only hope things would be improving soon.

Later that week, Johnny called me in to help untangle a small piece of confusion developing with another outfit that managed its business somewhat informally. Johnny said he needed to get a handle on an amount, $600,000 specifically, about which he had received a call from an investor syndicate on the East Coast trying to market some of his Eames, 3D seismic. I knew the outfit and so I said sure, I'll see what I can do. What I didn't know was that Johnny had already shown sample clips of the East Coast company's 3D seismic to another potential customer. I also didn't know that this East Coast investor had contacted another company to take a piece of the deal. So when East Coast realized they didn't have an exclusive on the deal, they went ahead and shot the remainder of a large piece of acreage which Johnny had under option. And then topped it off by turning around and charging Johnny $600,000 for their shoot. Granted, the charge was unauthorized. So when Johnny called them on it, they said it was all just paperwork to make them look good, since the obligation was being transferred to a wholly-owned subsidiary in the process of going public, and they needed to beef up the net worth on the subsidiary's records by adding to its accounts receivable. They told me this when I looked into it, and I later told Johnny not to worry because it would be taken care of down the road.

A couple of weeks later, a call came in from the East Coast syndicate's agent who said he needed to swing a deal in order to repay Johnny the $600,000 and that Johnny should be getting a draft for that amount wired directly to his bank. But, if his deal did not go through, Johnny was to return the money immediately, and he would send the money again when his next deal got put together.

Actually, Johnny did receive a draft for $600,000 soon after that call—his bank notified him of that fact. But later that same day, about 3p.m. in the afternoon, he got a long distance call saying the deal did not go through, and to return the $600,000 immediately. Johnny did so, discovering later that the $600,000 received was in their books as payment to them from Eames Seismic Technologies for the unauthorized shoot. This transaction was written on the books of the second seismic company, the first added $600,000 to the $1.2 million they wanted from Johnny as the estimated value of the 3D they had thought they were buying but did not receive. Basically, this accounted for the forced entry of the offices later on for search and seizure of $1.8 million cash and or hard assets approximating that value.

Meanwhile, Johnny was approached by the agent for the East Coast group once more who said if Johnny gave him all the necessary files and seismic concerning a contested shoot, which Texaco had put up the money for and with Johnny coming in for fifty percent down the line but was currently having second thoughts, and Texaco was suing—then he, the agent, would resolve the dispute and take his cut from the settlement and Johnny would be home free.

"Can we review here for a minute?"
"Sure, ask me anything."
"Not sure what to ask."

"Know what you mean."

"Well, go ahead, it'll straighten out, I'm sure."

OK, and so it went. Seismic company #1, British owned, American operated, claimed that Johnny owed them $600,000 for their completion of a shoot on some of Johnny's optioned acreage the previous August, the one Johnny said he never authorized.

Company #1 also said they had agreed to purchase $1.2 million 3D seismic from Johnny and Johnny had sent them the tapes for review but then they discovered Johnny had sold the same seismic for $1.7 million to an as yet undisclosed buyer. Johnny counter-claimed he had not sold #1 the original tapes, but only proofs of the shoot, that no agreement was ever reached, and that he knew nothing about the so-called undisclosed buyer. Meanwhile, Gary was safeguarding a strongbox full of original tapes until things cleared up.

So the seismic completed for $600,000 was involved and the seismic sold or not sold to the first party and simultaneously sold or not sold to a second party for $1.2 and the other deal mentioned for $1.7 million was beginning to start folks speculating.

When Johnny returned from another chartered sailboat two-week vacation in the Caribbean with Florence, suspicious tongues wagged about whether "missing funds" were probably stashed on one of the British Islands beyond the reach of U.S. authority.

A suit and then a judgment was entered against Johnny by the British-owned company, their claim being that they had purchased proprietary seismic from Eames Seismic Technologies who then turned around and sold it to a second party who had as yet not taken delivery on the seismic in question and made this known to the first party who cited this information in the suit. Just to complicate things, the global company went ahead and shot seismic on a large part of acreage Johnny held exclusively, and then billed Johnny $980,000 for the unauthorized seismic job. It was a downright act of privateering aggression. Johnny thought best to forget about it and do nothing because he had told them he had not authorized the job in the first instance.

"Would you gentlemen care for some dessert. Cherry cobbler, banana pudding?"
"Lester, the cobbler's the best anywhere!"
"I'm good."
"I'll have some of that cobbler."

Anyway, Johnny meanwhile sent samples of seismic film to a third party through the second party, on spec, payment on acceptance of deal, which went through, but he was told by the first party that selling that seismic at that time for $1.2 million was illegal. This seemed to explain the phone call Johnny had gotten telling him he was going to get a $600,000 payment but if the deal did not go through, he would have to return the money and he would then get it another way.

When this last action was reported to the UK company, it promptly flew off its corporate handle and got a judge to serve a search and seizure on Johnny's offices and home—

which explains the forced entry mentioned earlier—for assets to pay off what was now a Judgment, first for $600,000, but which would shortly climb to well over $2 million.

The Sheriff and his several deputies arrived one Thursday morning. Florence happened to be there at the time and sent out for doughnuts and served coffee to everyone, holding forth as if it was a party being held in her honor. It was a very appreciative group of men who, nevertheless, started down the hall to seize assets, files, and furniture. Hearing them coming, Johnny tossed Gary the entire set of original tapes of the contested 3D claimed to have been sold more than once. Gary shoved them into a plastic film bag and slipped out a back door to the parking lot, bought a metal safe box and stored the cassettes in a location only he and Johnny knew about. When the Sheriff was satisfied, he turned around and did the same at Johnny's home, removing computers and anything else that looked suspiciously like business-related elements.

Big Roy was downright disgusted at the turn of events and fumed about it violently every day. Chapter 11 declaration took place shortly thereafter and things turned into nightmare time.

As summer arrived, the Bankruptcy Judge came down and came down hard. He told Johnny that the $50,000 bonus he had given to his (ex-) partner, Big Roy, plus the $5,000 a month for two years, plus the equivalent leasing cost of the ground floor office suite down the hall *would have to be returned!* They said Big Roy's howling topped that of a

Woolly Mammoth mired in primeval mud being brought down by the spears of Clovis Indians! When he had gotten sufficient control of himself to handle the telephone, Roy had his lawyers initiate a massive lawsuit against his old friend, Johnny Eames.

Then the Judge told Johnny that he would have to get back the $110,000 he had given his lawyer as a vague retainer. Both money collections to be handled by Johnny's new bankruptcy lawyer, who was himself busy eating Johnny out of office and parking lot.

"Miss, could I have a little more of that cobbler? Lester?"

"Hmm, yes, I will try that banana pudding after all."

"Ok gentlemen, be right back."

I don't know, in for a buck, in for a million I guess. Johnny, who seemed to be really hurting by now for cash, proceeded to complicate things further, if you can believe it.

A longtime oil company owner, a client of Johnny's, brought over a bankrupt English geophysicist on condition that he work solely for his benefactor, Johnny's client, for 90 days to make up the cost of moving the Englishman's bankrupt staff and company from London to the U.S. Without sharing with Johnny any of the details of this arrangement, this English geophysicist, Elliot Foster, proceeded to enter into a partnership with Johnny, something expressly forbidden in Foster's contract, flying out to another oil-centered city to talk another company based there into opening a bank account for the Foster and Eames partnership, utilizing equipment owned by Foster's benefactor to shoot lines for themselves in that distant area.

All of this was being kept hopefully from another British-owned U.S.-based seismic hardware and software company who had agreed to install two of their seismic workstations in Johnny's offices, with the understanding that it would be available to other interested independents at discount rates which Johnny could use to help pay off the purchase of the two workstations. This did not work too well. The software had bugs yet to be worked out, the company was not well organized itself, and the paperwork and bookkeeping did not follow a schedule yet.

Business elements of this sort probably explained why the whole deal with three rooms of equipment was moved out of Johnny's offices two months after being installed. Cissie followed the equipment out, waving goodbye to all, and was replaced by a temp-secretary who knew nothing about the seismic industry, or bookkeeping, for that matter.

Johnny even reconsidered the oil and gas exploration partnership he and Gary had discussed from time to time, going so far as opening offices around the corner, saying it could work as long as Florence never got wind of it, and that what money Johnny put into the partnership would be out of his own pocket. He did take time to reassign to Gary, as a gesture of good will, rights to several thousand acres he had optioned to run seismic lines.

But things were moving swiftly and, even though one week earlier Gary had moved into the new offices around the corner and installed computers, desks, a variety of equipment and supplies so he and Johnny could pursue their plans, Johnny reluctantly told Gary that as of that moment any signed agreements were null and void. He would, however, look at any deals coming out of the sections that Gary had the right to run lines on, and that he would come in as a fifty-fifty partner if any looked promising. But Gary shook his head, having finally had his fill.

But I'm with Johnny. I believed him then and continue to believe him now. And that's why I want to see that Johnny gets what he deserves.

I nodded for the check.

"Listen Lester, what kind of money are you talking about anyway. A lot, a little…?"

"Why," he said, "the original six hundred thousand that Johnny was done out of."

I thought about a postcard I had received a while back from the boat-chartering agent Johnny always used, promoting the joys of sailing the Caribbean in a beautiful yacht—rent or lease to own, "for a vacation of a lifetime or a lifetime vacation." When I looked more carefully at the card a second time, the second "lifetime" seemed to have been faintly underlined.

I tried to picture what the pair was doing, in all probability, somewhere in the Caribbean at the moment. I could see Johnny cutting up dead fish on his cutting board resting on barrels, 'round the side of his bait shack on the beach under two palm trees, while Florence padded around in sandals and a wraparound flowered skirt and halter, serving warm beer to waiting bait customers at the three little tables out in front of the shack, snappishly responding that "there's no ice, the ice has not been delivered yet." That six hundred thousand would be welcome indeed because they could then pay off the fisherman they owed for the daily fish supply, the landlord for his shack, and the beer distributor who had carried them for over two months at that point.

Lester and I walked out of the restaurant onto the sidewalk together. Lester gave me his card and asked me to contact him immediately if I ever heard anything further about Johnny Eames.

But as I watched him drive off toward the Interstate, I was having second thoughts myself. I was beginning to strongly suspect that the $600,000 reimbursement story was simply a way of luring Johnny up from the deeps of whatever waters he had slipped into.

Johnny never did show again. Wiped his tracks clean, not a trace or a whisper of him or his helpmate.

But we have to have a winner emerge from the pit once in awhile or what would the rest of us have to believe in? Certainly Johnny had done nothing to anyone they had not tried to do to him. Had not the loss of everything, including his home, meant that he had more than paid his dues?

The picture I prefer to have when I think of Johnny and Florence is the two of them holding forth on the afterdeck of their schooner *Seismic Wanderer* without a care in the world, with several million in funds well invested, which earned them, via Switzerland, a comfortable check each month. The game of oil being a shade more punishing than Vegas gaming tables, luck plays a most critical role. Master swindler or well-meaning salesman, I think Johnny's luck held and he and Florence lived out their days in a style they soon grew accustomed to and in a setting they had always thoroughly enjoyed.

JUST LOOKING

Clarice and her brother grew up in a two-bedroom clapboard frame house between the railroad tracks and the Wrenfroe river. Before she was five, Clarice could dig for worms, get to the end of their little dock, and catch the first catfish every time before her older brother even got situated.

Later, afternoons were spent on bikes or playing ball in the open field about a mile south of her house, a game fiercely fought by a gang of tough kids where she was the only girl, although nobody noticed.

When it came time to move up into high school years, it was not easy to abandon jeans and shirts for dresses and sweaters but there was a strictly enforced dress code. Clarice had few friends and Pat Knowles was her best one. She and Pat matriculated together and Pat went off on a basketball scholarship where, six years later, she had earned a Masters in Business Administration and returned to her hometown to take a local assistant manager's job. Clarice's bent was toward the technical, computer studies, not exactly fulfilling a well-secured worm dangling in front of an unsuspicious catfish, but still, it meant working on her own which she always preferred when it was possible. Before long, she had joined the branch of a large computer firm where she kept busy staying abreast of the continuous innovations in information technology systems.

This much Allen knew from what she had told him over early morning breakfasts and occasional oriental lunches. He knew she was single, although she mentioned a certain Pat now and then; he knew she was smart, her work with the computer firm was highly specialized; and he knew her well-built strong body hidden under tailored suits, included some very interesting curves. He was not on the prowl himself for a life companion. No plans, not for awhile. But when the time came, he would definitely put Clarice on the preferred list. He knew what was lying in wait under those trim jackets and slightly slit skirts, because Clarice had begun a little routine of hugging when they parted in the parking lot outside the breakfast restaurant when it came time for her to go on to work. She had developed a fondness for Allen over the two years they had known each other but could not tell for certain where he was going to wind up. Allen was a freelance person managing to live on deals he put together and sold for cash or participation. But his real love was the design of delivery systems, upper management level, for manufacturing firms. He had been referred to Clarice as someone who would be best to know how the big computer corporation, with operations all over the world, could be of any help to him. She studied and marveled at some of his graphics and provided him with contacts, which he eventually followed up on.

One evening when the holidays were approaching, they went out to dinner at a very special Chinese restaurant. There, their table blocked by screens, she told him about a recent national corporate conference she had just returned from. He listened thoughtfully but at the same time really studied her face for the first time. Her short-cropped dark hair framed a searching look that proclaiming all the information she had gathered and retained for him could not belie. Allen wondered what, beyond the usual coupling, that searching look reflected. She had mentioned leasing a small house with a roommate, but from the way she talked, there did not seem to be any intimacy about the arrangement.

They ate slowly and had several glasses of a special house liqueur. She said she wanted to tell him something but preferred a little more privacy. They went out to the emptying parking lot and got in her car. She lit a cigarette, which was not her custom or habit.

"Last week," she began, "I was driving to work and I noticed a woman with two young children in the car in front of me. They were jumping around, and the woman who was trying to drive smacked the two kids every time traffic slowed. They kept it up until she stopped for a traffic light and gave them both a series of hard slaps. I was irritated and then upset about what I was watching. I followed her car to a school where the two kids jumped out and fled into the building.

"Then I followed the car again until the woman drove through the parking lots of a large mall, found a place, gave herself a quick going over in the rear view mirror and got out. I followed her into the mall and down the walkways to a gift shop which she entered. I stayed outside the doors of the shop while she went in the back, hung up her coat and came out on the floor. I pretended to be just looking at the displays in the shop's windows but studied her covertly. I thought about things that could happen to that woman. I thought about making her disappear and afterward, how it would be if I took her place. I thought about taking her place and caring for those two kids and being the one to drive them to school. I thought about it so long, I was startled when someone next to me said, 'They have some nice things in there but they certainly are on the high side.'

"Brought back to the moment, I nodded and stepped away and walked back to my car. When I put the key in the ignition, I was still trembling from where I had been and what I had been thinking."

They both sat in silence for a little bit, Clarice lost in recalling the intense experience, Allen wondering if this was fantasy, dream, or worse, a woman stalking a child abuser and considering her demise?

Allen reached over and held Clarice for a little bit. A natural envelope of intensified intimacy surrounded the moment. But Allen was uneasy, she had revealed a side of herself that he was not too excited to pursue. Not so much thinking what she thought, but actually stalking another person? How normal is that, he thought.

He had to be traveling then for several weeks and it was midwinter before he called her number just to touch base.

"Hey Clarice, how's every little thing?"

"Been awhile, you doing all right?"

"Oh sure, what are you up to anyway?"

"Cooking catfish, matter of fact, you like catfish? We have them about once a week."

"Sure I like catfish, always have."

"Would you like to come over some evening and share the next batch?"

"Absolutely."

There was some covered conversation.

"Are you free next week, say Wednesday evening?"

"Well, let's do it, then." She gave him the address and how to find the place, they chatted a bit longer and then said their good-byes.

He arrived punctually with a bottle of light white wine. Clarice came out of the kitchen and gave him a stiff little hug. Behind him, at the far end of the living room, a log fire was burning brightly. Leaning on the mantelpiece was a lanky youthful person who nodded in Allen's direction but did not move. She took him by the arm, ushered him to the end of the living room and said, "This is Pat, remember my telling you about her back when she was made vice president of marketing of this whole region?"

Pat smiled and they shook hands firmly. She had played a good bit of high school and college basketball, her favorite thing to do after marketing for chain store systems, she said winking.

So Clarice had resolved her longing and she and Pat had set up house together and that was about that. He noticed she was no longer her trim self and had begun to put on weight. She was making herself over in front of Allen. All through the evening, which was pleasant enough, she bustled about, not allowing Pat to be bothered to do anything but chat with Allen and play Barbra Streisand tapes for him.

The attractive independent look and thought had dissolved into an acquiescing housewife disguise. They ate dinner, formally set and served in a small dining room. Clarice jumped up and down with many trips to the kitchen; Allen and Pat talked business statistics, the economy, and the future of franchise operations. Saying goodbye, Clarice stood stalwartly by Pat's side while everyone shook hands and promised to do it again soon.

A year later he did not recognize Clarice until she practically had to shout "Allen" when they crossed paths in a local store one afternoon. He complimented her on how well she looked, trying not to notice the continuing weight gain.

Clarice had opened a niche for one night only at her home shared with Pat and he knew he would never see her again except accidentally, like this chance meeting.

The searching had been replaced by a protective complacency.

Allen realized then that the venture she had shared with him had not been a dream, or a fantasy, or anything else; it had been a warning, created for Clarice in a language she could understand and heed or not. In heeding, she had chosen a childless life that would never allow what she considered to be the darker, as well as uncontrollable side of herself, to surface again.

BORDER TOWN

It was tempting, it really was. He had finished early, oil leases signed, a very successful trip, what harm in a couple of cold ones across the border? Couple of cold ones, always a chance for a little excitement, then hit the highway and be back in the city in a few short hours of nighttime driving. Saturday morning, too, he could sleep in. He deserved a little R & R and that settled it.

He deliberated about driving his truck across the bridge into the sprawling border town and decided to park it on the U.S. side, because what could happen to himself was far less important than having anything happen to that truck. He found a spot not too far from the bridge, disconnected and hid the cell phone and its umbilical cord and the radar warning device on the floor in the back with a couple of horse blankets thrown over to cover the tool box as well.

Then he got out, looked carefully around, noted a couple of landmarks and walked the three blocks to the bridge. It was outlined in a smoky glare of sunset, no rain for weeks created a permanent layer of fine dust everywhere which was kicked up through the day, covering the many vehicles lined up and the dozens of *trabajadores*, their *mujeres* and *ninos* who trod those steps from Mexico to the U.S. and back every day for what little work they could find—a dusty two-way caravan of flowing humanity. Now he was part of it.

The streets on the Mexican side of the river crossing made do between rainy seasons, when they would become deeply pocked with mud holes, the underlayment of the curbing laid bare to crumble, the white-washed walls cracked and stained and covered with layers of posters advertising the good life. Most of the bars were no more than a ten or twelve-foot room with a counter and refrigerator and a radio blaring. He paused at the end of a little square with benches and blooming bushes and a small fountain burbling in the middle. Then he headed diagonally across the plaza toward a tavern on the far side.

There were several customers at the long bar and a few scattered at tables. He ordered a beer. It was cold and he drank the first bottle without putting it down.

"What's your name?" a man on his left looked at him, half-smiling.

"Weaver," he said, "and yours?"

"Carlos, Carlos Manotes, amigo, what you drinking there, Weaver, hmm?"

"Beer."

"*Por hay*, beer, you need better. Pachuco, his name is Pachuco, friend of mine, Pachuko," he said to the bartender, "bring us a bottle of your best Mesc*al, por favor*.

We get ready for the women, you and I, huh?" he laughed and shook his head and poured two shots of the Mescal. Weaver thought about women. It had been awhile.

"Where you from, hombre, Tejas?"

Weaver nodded. It was easier. "Where you from, Carlos?"

"Tlaxapan, fifty *mass o menos* miles south, like a bird, south. I have a ranch for breeding horses. That is where my family lives."

"Horses? What you doin' up here, buyin' horses?"

"No, no, no…comin' through from Chicago…I work in construction in Chicago for six months, carpenter foreman, the best, and the best money too, then I head south for six months to my family and my horses. Just coming through, is all, and headed home now until spring, until weather breaks up north again."

They drank from the bottle, and the night turned the little park outside into a gathering place for those looking for love. Streetlights had blinked on, the bumper to bumper traffic had thinned down. He looked around for Carlos who was just returning from the rest room.

"So you like horses, too, huh, Weaver? What kind you got?"

He thought about his string two or three hundred miles to the northwest of that bar, munching alfalfa tonight, contented in their box stalls that bordered the training track.

"Race horses," he said. He looked across the large room and focused on a hallway where he had seen his friend disappear.

"Be right back," and he pushed off concentrating very hard on walking without staggering, and he thought he was doing it very convincingly until he came up hard against the corner of the hallway entrance. He backed off, patted the plaster, laughed to himself, and proceeded under better control to the door marked Caballeros. It was crowded inside and when a urinal became empty he focused on moving there, but not without bumping somebody enroute. He started to relieve himself when someone hit his shoulder. He ignored it, finishing what he was doing when there was a second hit, this time no mistaking it for an accident.

"I'm talking to you, hombre, hey, you no hear me?"

He zipped up and turned around. A short stocky Mexican was standing behind him caressing his fist in his other palm. "Who you think you are, comin' in here and runnin' into people and not saying you're sorry or nothin'?"

"Sorry man, didn't see you," and he pushed toward the door. The little man would not give way and his friends saw an opportunity to have some fun with this gringo.

"What you do?"

"Horses," he said, thinking that would be simplest to understand.

"Horses? Let me see your hands," and he grabbed Weaver's hands and turned them palm up.

"You a liar, man," he said, repeating it to his friends, his black eyes glittering, "he's a liar, look at his hands, soft, like a woman's, he no work with horses, maybe you work with CIA, a CIA bastard!"

His two friends pressed in, looking for a kill. "You know what we do to CIA bastards over here? We do them so they never come back, you hear what I'm sayin' to you, cabron?"

One of the men grabbed his arm and another gave him a push back. "What's the matter with you guys, huh? Came in here not looking for trouble and now you say I'm a CIA spy? You're crazy, man, I'm just here for a couple of drinks and then I go back, is all."

"Lying bastard," the short man heard what he was waiting to hear, that non-aggressive note in the voice, could be right on the edge of fear. But Weaver knew he could not afford to show any fear or he would be dead before he ever left that rest room. He couldn't help choking out a laugh when he thought of his epitaph "Suspected Undercover Agent Dead in the Head".

"You think this is funny, you CIA bastard," and suddenly they were all locked together and shoving back and forth in the rest room like four drunken sailors on the deck of a pitching ship. He got a couple of good swings in, connecting with the short man's ear and sending him down to his knees for a moment. Then he took a crash over his eye and felt blood run down, then a fine cut along the ribs under his arm from a switch blade and then another just over his eye and he knew it was deadly serious. He knew he had to focus and focus hard now to get out of there alive. So he attacked, plunging in, striking out blindly and kicking as viciously as he could. He knew he landed a few but he was up against a flailing deadly windmill of six arms and six feet and he did not know how long he could last in there. Suddenly, there was a shot. Everything came to a halt like a freeze frame. Carlos was putting his gun back in his belt under the back of his jacket.

"What the hell is goin' on here, ninos?"

"This is a CIA cabron and we need to kill the son of a bitch right now!"

Carlos moved into the group aggressively, taking Weaver's arm in his fist.

"This guy is my friend. He has horses, he's no CIA man, he's with me, stand back 'fore you make the biggest mistake of your life. I mean it, don't mess with me…"

They stood back.

"Come on Weaver, let's get the hell out of here if you're finished doing what you came in to do," and he lead Weaver away, and through the Caballeros door which closed slowly on three angry faces.

"Here, drink up, let's go find some women, hombre," he said to Weaver's back at the bar. "Pachuco, give us a clean rag…there, that's better," he said, daubing at Carlos' eye. The whole episode had not lasted fifteen minutes but it seemed like he and his friend had known each other for many years. He left some dollars on the bar and followed Carlos out onto the dark street where Carlos hailed a cab by stepping in front of it and motioning Weaver to go ahead and get in and then climbed in behind him and shouted something to the driver.

"Where we goin?"

"We goin where there is girls, lots of girls, nothing but girls my friend. Boys Town it's called."

"How far?"

"Not far."

They soon were out of the dusty town on a road that seemed like paved waves. Up and down, up and down, until Weaver thought, "If this damn highway doesn't flatten out soon I'm jumping overboard." But then a few lights grew into many lights, they rolled onto narrow streets brightly lit, clean sidewalks and little cafes, like a wonderland of nightclubs in a Hollywood backlot.

"Here, stop here," and Carlos paid off the driver and they got out. The first two clubs they peered into were empty. Then Carlos found a friend at the bar of the third place and went on in for a few minutes while Weaver enjoyed the clear night air.

Carlos came out and said, "We're early, that's it, too early, but there's some action at the Palacio around the corner."

Inside the Palacio the jukebox was blaring. Some regulars were hunched over the bar, a few early customers sat here and there at tables with women dressed in fancy evening dresses. There must have been about twelve women in the room when Weaver had gotten his bearings and looked around.

"Here, Weaver, sit, sit here, *ola, chiquitas, ven aqui, ven agui*," and several women detached themselves and drifted smiling over to the table where Carlos and Weaver were sitting.

"Drinks for the ladies," Carlos shouted to the bar-tender and a waiter soon came hurrying over with cham-pagne glasses filled with what could have been pink lemonade. When the waiter waited for payment, Carlos shouted, "Put it on the tab, we'll get it later," but not be-fore Weaver heard him say, bending over to Jorge, "Fifty dollars, Señor," and Weaver mentally registered what a fifty-dollar round in this place was going to add up to in a few hours, but joined Carlos in clinking his beer bottle to the ladies.

The place was slowly filling up. Several couples out on the floor dancing now. Carlos was enjoying the attention of three or four women who fussed over him and laughed at everything he was saying. But Weaver's eye was caught by a smaller female who was dancing each number with the same customer. Might have been a relative for she was not trying to make any moves on him. Her black hair was worn loosely to her shoulders, a simple light blue tailored dress outlined her petite figure. Once or twice Weaver thought she was looking straight at him. After the music ended, she walked back to the bar by herself, pulling her-self up onto a stool next to a girl friend. Weaver got up from the table and walked over to the bar where she was sitting.

He tapped her lightly on the shoulder. "Hey," he said when she turned around, "my name is Weaver. You like to dance?" he motioned toward the dance floor. Her dark hair framed a very pretty face and he felt strongly drawn toward her, just standing there. His eye must have been bleeding again because she sucked in her breath, leaned over the bar to rummage in her bag and came back with a couple of tissues. She called to the bartender and he gave her a handful of ice which she tightly wrapped and pressed onto the cut. In a moment the bleeding had stopped.

"What's your name?" he asked her.

She slid off the stool and took him by the hand and led him to the dance floor. "Aviva," she said in his ear, when they began to slow dance. "Aviva," he murmured. They moved easily together. She wore a fragrant scent faintly mindful of flowers of some sort. Her breasts and pelvis seemed to be an extension of his own body without particularly pressing against him. The music stopped then and he led her back to the bar.

Carlos was yelling, "Hey, Weaver, get back here, I got too much you know what for one hombre, hombre!" Weaver walked across the crowded room to rejoin his friend. By now others had pulled up to this table of endless refreshments. Weaver noted about eight men and women who had not been there before, lustily enjoying the situation with everything but party hats on. There was food on the table and he helped himself to a tamale.

"*Le gusta esta muchacha,* Weaver? Hey?" Carlos shouted at him above the local din, raising his head toward the bar. "Sweet, hmm, like a ripe mango, hmm?" he laughed pouring some mescal out and handing it down the table toward Weaver.

Yes, Aviva was sweet, very sweet, and very seductive. He glanced in her direction but could not see her through the crowd. Somehow he knew she would not be joining this table full of rabble-rousers tonight. He also noted with alarm that Carlos was spending money like it was a never-ending stream straight from the vaults of Chicago. He also knew that Carlos would expect him to ante up before the night was over. Finally, he knew he did not have that kind of money on him, would never carry that much with him on a night like this across the border. But what was hidden safely in his truck was not going to help him out here. He laughed toward Carlos and raised the glass of mescal and got up and found Aviva again. He did not have to say anything. As soon as she saw him, she got up and met him halfway and they pushed their way to the dance floor.

"I missed you, Aviva," he said half jokingly as they began to dance. Her left hand went up around his neck and she stroked the back of his head in answer. "I want to be with you," he said. She nodded without looking at him. "No, no, I mean for a time, *por un tiempo*."

"*Que que?*" she asked, now pulling back and watching his face.

"Where are you from?"

"Guadalajara. My brothers and sisters live in a small town south of Guadalajara. My mother is sick. That is why I am working up here. But I am not allowed to spend more than an hour or so with a customer."

"Let me take you to Guadalajara for the weekend. We could get a hotel room and be together for two or three days." Weaver had a growing desire to do just that with Aviva who seemed to be more seductively beautiful each time he danced with her.

"I would lose my job and I can't afford to lose it or I could not send money home to my mother and brothers and sisters."

Oh boy, Weaver thought. "Well, what would your boss charge for you to go with me to Guadalajara for the weekend?"

"A hundred dollars a day he would charge."

Funny, but at that point Weaver's heart sank. Not that he didn't have the money, at least he had it stashed in his truck. But, as beautiful as she was, he was disappointed that he would be expected to pay some guy for her company especially when he knew there was a strong attraction they shared for each other. After the dance ended, they drifted back to Carlos' party table.

"Hey, compadre, don't think about leaving until we settle this bill, ok?" Carlos looked like a nice guy but Weaver remembered how quickly that gun had come out in the restroom earlier and how easily he had used it. And he knew it was still shoved under his belt underneath his jacket. So he smiled and nodded. "Don't worry about it, my friend," and Carlos looked away satisfied. But when he took Aviva by the hand and led her through the outer, less crowded rooms, and seemed to be headed for the main entrance, Carlos was there in a flash, smiling broadly, putting his hand heavily on Weaver's shoulder.

"Getting some fresh air, amigo?"

"Nope, just thinking about finding a spot for me and my fiancé here, you know what I mean?"

"Forget about it, these girls aren't allowed to sleep with customers except by special arrangement with the boss. They're really just to get the booze flowing, comprende?"

The three of them walked back to the central hall and to the table. Then Weaver got up and danced with Aviva again.

"I need to leave," he whispered in her ear. "I will come back for you and we will go to Guadalajara and be together and visit your sick mother and brothers and sisters…but I need to leave here for now and soon." He looked around. It always seemed that Carlos was just looking up to spot him.

"I understand, my darling, but you will come back, for sure?"

"Yes, oh yes, you can count on it."

At that moment Carlos got up and headed toward the men's rest room. Weaver saw his chance and took it. He squeezed Aviva, stepped back from her, held her chin in his hand for a long moment, kissed her forehead and told her to go back to the table for a few minutes Then he headed through the crowd walking slowly but directly toward the main entrance while Carlos was occupied. He knew he only had two or three minutes to get out of the building…and then out of sight of the building's entrance way. His heart pounded, his throat was dry, his head throbbed. Bad enough with all the mescal, the fear of what Carlos might do when he discovered him skipping out drove him mindlessly forward. He did not want to run and attract attention but he had to get to a corner and turn before Carlos figured out he had taken off and came looking for him. If he had had the money he wouldn't have minded. But that Mexican carpenter was incorrigible, ordering round after round for all those people who had flocked to his table. It could easily have added up to more than a thousand dollars. No, he had to escape, all there was to it.

He reached the corner and started jogging down a darker street. Fortunately, the block was not too long. When he came to the next intersection it was not much better lighted. He thought he saw the lights of a taxi about four blocks down and waited anxiously, but at the last moment it turned out of sight. He realized that the street the Palacio was on was probably the main drag and that not too much was happening on these side streets. He jogged nervously four blocks which would put him well past the Palacio entrance. Then he turned right again and approached the main street cautiously. He went no further than the end of the corner, staying in the shadows just in case. In a few minutes a cab came cruising by. "Hey! Cab!" he shouted sharply. The cabbie hit his brakes and Weaver ran quickly out into the well-lighted wide street and jumped in.

"Go!" he urged the driver.

"Donde, Señor?"

"Just go...back to town...hombre, go!" He hunched down in the back seat, peering over, dreading what he might see, but there was no one in sight. The driver moved slowly down the street.

"Por favor, hombre, mas rapido!"

They took the humpety humps at a pretty good clip and Weaver wondered if he was going to throw up. When they got to the bridge, he offered the driver ten extra dollars to take him across. Once on the other side, he paid up and walked the three blocks after waiting for the cab to turn around and return to Mexico. When the cab was out of sight, he headed off for his truck which he had parked about three blocks into town.

At the edge of the city, the lights of an all-night burger joint made him realize he had not eaten that day. He pulled in, ordered two to go, and continued driving out of the city.

Once out on the interstate again, he drove until he came to a rest area, pulled in, ate his two burgers savagely, then fell over and slept, dreaming anxiously of meeting Aviva at the train station for their journey to Guadalajara.

CAREER DAY

Good morning, good morning, just take any seat...Hello there...yes, any seats, let me open these blinds just a bit...There...is that everyone?

"Ah yes, you're probably the last one; would you close the door for me? Thank you.

"Good.

"Well...my name is on the board as you can see—Mr. Rodzuzrinski...you have been guided here during this, your day of registration, to this little meeting room because, apparently, you have yet to select your minor, oddly enough, at this late date, in the early spring registration here at this famous school of performing arts. Yes?"

"But I want to be a bookkeeper."

"Fine, you belong in B, next room down the hall. This room is A for arts.

"All right then...My function today is to elaborate for you some facts and features about various kinds of arts activities, and something about the artists that bring them to life, and perhaps something about the various kinds of audiences one may be confronted with before your respective careers have been completed, in the hope that—if you are not too discouraged by my remarks, and I certainly hope you are not, that you will have a clearer picture from which to make your complementary course of training, complementary to your major which I assume you have been engaged with for a very long time.

"Now then, excuse me?"

"What is that pointer in your hand for?"

"This?"

"Yes."

"This is not a pointer; this is an orchestral conductor's baton."

"Why do you carry it around?"

"Hmm? Well, that's because I am a conductor, studying conducting, graduate work, conducting work, graduate level. I *like* to carry it with me because it reminds me in between times when I'm not conducting, that it doesn't really count, sort of thing."

"What can *I* carry around so 'in between' doesn't count?"

"You're very good, quick. Enough, I haven't the slightest idea how we got there. Well, I *hope* this session counts, for *you*, that is, you really need to think about this choice right now!

"So let's proceed, where was I? Oh, yes...

"Incidentally, you may have noticed the posters around the room of different artists doing their respective thing...

"Go ahead, look now...

"We may also look at some film clips of more of the same if we have any time left this morning...

"I know it looks a little Rorschachty but it is not twin butterflies, those two are doing something in a work called Copellia,…Hmm? Well, he is *lifting* her…yes, to help her move safely through the air.

"No, you don't want to try that sort of thing with a friend without a couple of basics.

"Let's start with the general and then consider the specific…

"I'll just write this on the board."

The Arts

Some Aspects

Let's just think about the arts for a moment. What can we say about them? Hmm?

Rhetorical, exactly. Now then…

I will suggest that…they are not easily grouped together.

They are not often found in a healthy growing condition.

They are not products of an assembly line…or of a corporation…or of a city council…or of an educational institution, for that matter.

They are not dissectible.

I mean to say that they cannot be taken apart and put back together and resemble anything near what they started out to be.

They are not alike.

They are not the same size.

They do not have the same requirements to happen.

They are not the same age.

They do not have the same parents, necessarily...or grandparents...or ancestors in common for that matter. Then again, they might.

They require years of training.

This does not stop those without years of training to go right ahead.

Usually, the public tends to sort out who has had sufficient training and who hasn't.

But—you say, and rightly so, how can you tell a professional from—well, you know, someone who may not count?

How can you do that and be really sure?

A fair question about which there is much confusion and I will be glad to straighten out the whole matter.

Let me just erase THE ARTS and write this on the board.

The Professional

Some Clear Facts

After all, you *are* applying to an institution which, above all, is dedicated to the development and eventual highly regarded professional product.

So let's see what that means exactly, hmm, well...a professional cannot necessarily be recognized by the layperson.

Or by another professional.

He or she may not work at his or her profession full time.

Just half time.

Or one half day a week.

Or seasonally.

A professional may be someone with several degrees.

Or someone without any degrees.

When the individual is not working, it is about the same thing for both those with degrees and those without.

Working, for some, means doing the thing they have trained themselves to do.

Working, for others, means teaching what they have trained themselves to do.

When the thing is a dog act, everyone knows whether you are doing it, teaching it, or are simply between bookings.

When the thing involved is composing, no one knows what you are doing, ever.

It's a case of being better off seen and not heard.

On the other hand, a composer can compose and simply never be performed.

Whereas, a choreographer cannot do much without bodies.

As it works out in real life, this simply means that there are far fewer choreographers around than composers.

In this instance, it is a case of being better off heard from but not seen.

A conductor is best off of all for he only needs a score, a stand, a baton, a full-length mirror and a recording of his favorite symphonic work.

Unless he happens to have an orchestra.

Most instrumentalists, however, are not as well off by themselves as a conductor.

Just walk down any corridor of any musical training institution that has practice rooms available and listen for yourself.

An actor has it made because he can simply go into his thing on any street corner. Trouble is, the passerby is never sure whether the actor is on or not. This is possibly why so many actors develop such a lovely variety of neuroses, they are no longer sure themselves.

A mime is part dancer, part actor, part mute, part imitator—if things didn't happen in the world everyday on their own, the mime would be out of work even when he had work.

There are any number of additional facts about recognizing the professional but they tend toward the obscure.

So…now that we are pretty sure what the arts are not all about, we can proceed to inquire into who these artists might be…

Well, think of painters, poets, and flauting flutists,
dancers, singers, mimists, and collage constructionists,
filmmakers, conductors, and sculptors of dialogue, playwrights, dramatists, sculptors of wood, of stone, of bronze, sculptors of sound,

composers and banjo pickers,
ceramacists and potters,
jugglers and finger painters,
fine brush painters, bucket hurlers,

(oh yes, there was that one young lady in Paris who filled balloons with paint, covered them with plaster, shaped the plaster into the figure of a man, dragged the whole affair out into the yard behind her studio, loaded a small cannon, ignited the small cannon which fired a cannon ball fifty feet into the poor chap who bleeds mightily and in incredible Technicolor!),

    designers of pop art, designers of optical art,
designers of topographical art,
    acoustic guitarists, multi-media-ists, cross-hill
and dale-ists,
    jazz artists, folk artists, ethnic and blues artists,
    country western rock crossovers,
    actors and clowns and aerialists and sawyers,
    cellists, bell pullers and harpsichording
keyboardists,
    ballet dancers, classical ballet Balanchine
dancers,
    interpretive electronic ballet dancers, jazz and
folk ballet dancers,
    tap dancers and gymnasts, baton twirlers and
martial artists,
    non-martial artists,

whoever can beat and whatever can be beaten on…whoever can pull and whatever can be pulled…

whoever can pluck and whatever can be plucked…

hit at…colored, stuck together, fragmented, shot, filmed, discussed and disseminated,

hung…framed…mounted…exhibited… spaced…placed…and laced with love…

…if it's provocative, well executed, and has a distinctive voice—that's who!

All right then, how about a seventh inning stretch? Let's take five, but we need to regroup promptly, for the rest of this briefing…

Aren't you going to take a little walk with the others?

"I have a question."

"What's your question?"

"What about an audience?"

"The audience? A very good question. Well, there's just no way to get around the fact that the professional artist needs an audience. Nothing can replace live human bodies—just sitting out there. No canned sounds can duplicate the excitement of instantaneous response. However, for some, any busy intersection will do, if nothing else presents itself first, that is."

"He took my seat."

"He what? Oh, say, young man, just take the same seat again if you don't mind, hurry along, people."

"Don't you ever put that baton down? You might poke somebody, you know."

"No, I never put my baton down, and I don't *know* why.

"Have you been here all your life?"

"Not exactly but I have been studying here for some-time, fifth year in graduate orchestral conducting work, actually…

"If you check the board, you'll see I have replaced the focus of the earlier part of this meeting to…

The Audience

Some Understandings

"Everyone who has or is in any way responsible for the delivery of the arts knows full well that the best audience is a captive audience.

"A captive audience is not necessarily members of an active military installation halfway around the world.

"Or the inmates of a maximum-security prison—although these are two excellent examples of guaranteed highly demonstrable enthusiasm forthcoming regardless of how poor the quality of entertainment..

"A captive audience can be three hundred third and fourth graders marching into a cafetorium in single file.

"It can also be three thousand adults marching into a gorgeous hall in single file.

"It can also be two hundred patient business persons covertly checking their watches now that lunch is over and the soprano and her accompanist are now arranging the music for a fourth number.

"Mr. Rodzuzrinski?"

"Ah, Ms. Donaldson, do come in, a moment longer, we...are just entering the home stretch, you could say, I think.

"The real reason a captive audience is coveted by the professional performing artist is that whether it is a nightclub or a classroom, it means that the artist can go into a *set piece*. A *set piece* is work that has been rehearsed to perfection, hopefully, and once it is initially triggered, it is on its way to completion, no matter what!

"Most of what the larger performing ensembles do is technically complex and demands the *set piece* type of approach.

"It is often breathtaking to watch or to hear.

"Part of the viewer's excitement comes from the fact that should the *set piece* get in trouble, it has all the maneuverability of a glacier, which could create disaster in slow motion!"

"Like the Titanic?"

"Absolutely right. No way but down.

"However, there has always been a parallel over the centuries to the *set piece* approach.

"Those that follow this second persuasion are wandering, roving, make-it-upper-seat-of-the-pantsers, happy people, by and large, called minstrels, storytellers, jazz artists, folk singers, and late night TV talk show hosts.

"In order to enjoy this kind of freedom (distinguished from the *set piece* style), they develop a semi—sometimes quasi—sometimes just plain improvisational approach because they must create their audiences *on the spot.*

The site might be a county fair,
Or a crowded street corner,
A mall, a park, a playground...
But it can also be a gym, or a church
basement,
Or a gilded hall with ceilings out of sight and
magnificent chandeliers,
Because it is more of an attitude
Than a performing requirement!
It is a playing off an audience as you go along,
a sharing,
A particular event for everyone, and both
kinds of performers are needed, yes they are, so
that the non-captive audience is indeed,
captivated...and the captive audience feels free
to stay as long as they wish.

"And now I am certain that all of you have stayed as long as you wished...

"So, that's it, my part is done."

"Is that your orchestra down the hall?"

"Well, in a way, you see, as long as I can keep from graduating, it's my orchestra! And that's very rare, very rare, indeed, for a conductor these days.

"And now, Ms. Donaldson? Ms. Donaldson is going to escort you back down to the Registrar's office to complete your registration."

"Form a line along the wall, please, young people, and no talking."

"Good bye, my young friends, good bye, thank you for your kind attention—and good luck!"

MOs OF THE HUMAN ANIMAL

Any organization's volunteer board is no less than a microcosm of shared interest in a community activity focused on nearly always for more than a month, rarely longer than fifteen years, to do something that furthers the expressed common interest. Enough about structure.

The individuals who profess this need to share, however, come from very distinct, differing, biases.

To know the modus operandi, the method of operating, of a given human animal (we are all gloriously created animals, although the human species may be the most curious), is to know the potential orientation of the individual's response guideposts.

We do not hesitate to pursue the study of tigers, for knowing what and when and how they eat, can determine whether the tiger or the hunter goes home with the trophy.

So let us proceed with this inquiry with due diligence for one never knows, there may be, after all, a tiger among us.

A few examples to begin.

THE POLITICAL ANIMAL   He gathers steam with existing conditions that grow well outside of his sphere of influence; he is prone to a daily tally on where everyone else is going and tries to project the advantages of being there first; he will want you to believe that he is a standard bearer above and beyond but he is not *really* subject to any imposed (self/institutional/traditional) operating values, only in what is doable and has an edge.

Best to check this one out before you decide on whether he is friend or foe—he has already done the same about you—several times.

THE BUSINESS ANIMAL pans for opportunity in economic realms like the old-time gold prospectors and if none is sniffed out, moves on to more likely prospects; sole guideline concerns depth and productivity of the vein.

THE EDUCATING ANIMAL can hardly hear information before passing it on via subjective interpolation; gossip comes out theory, the hypothetical returns as fact, rumination as assumption; an information beagle hound, she stacks up her bits so that she can measure them out accurately after she has decided how many you deserve to receive; her whole bag being rearrangement, there is no turnabout, she wants anything you have to say to be literal and uncorrupted by such as the roving fingers of her mind.

THE HEALING ANIMAL   The Dr. Fixit of humanity, she looks at you in terms of how badly you need her, never *whether* you do or not; the body is abused, according to her standard, by everyone so you are on her list of potential patients before she has met you or been contacted; the body, what we like to think of as extraordinarily personal, is her garage, a place to putter in, a place where things can be cut up, taken apart and, hopefully, reassembled; if it hurts, he or she has a prescription drug for the occasion with absolutely minimal side effects.

THE REFERENCING ANIMAL   He does not care what or how you do what you do but is vitally concerned on where it has been written down that you should do whatever you do at all; if it is in the book, you're alright with him; if not, there will be no justification, as far as he's concerned, for anything you do.

THE TARGETING ANIMAL   She aims to achieve whatever she has decided is good for her to achieve and so, when she shoots, she shoots straight and only aims for the end result of all her efforts; she is not troubled by procedures, waiting in line, means to be employed, other animals, or popular or unpopular support; there is to be no interference, she is only concerned with what she has on her mind for the hunt today.

THE NESTING ANIMAL   Watch out for your situation, this one may be in it tomorrow instead of you; this one cannot construct a situation for himself so he is on the lookout for any prospect he can move into that has already been developed, has all the bugs out, and is working in tip top shape—that will do very nicely, and thank you! It need not be a place or a relationship, it may be a social situation or a political one, but whatever, the important thing to the nester is that it be prefabricated and suitable for his current interests.

THE RELIGIOUS ANIMAL   All things and all manifestation of things he puts into his predetermined order and evaluates accordingly; if he stoops a bit, it is not age but because the stone tablets inscribed with the Commandments weigh heavily on his shoulders, having been placed there many years ago by himself; he is much like the healing animal except he does not get actively involved with your 'abused' body, targeting your conscience instead with the assumption that, similarly, it too has been badly abused and will need much of his time in counseling as to how to find a way to redeem things.

THE CONSERVING ANIMAL   She waits for you to do your thing and then offers to keep it for you; while you are out doing your second thing, she leases your first thing to someone willing to pay double the price for it, explaining it all to you afterward when you come back with your second thing in tow—but your first now well out of hand—that it is the only way to run a bank.

And there are many more. See if you can spot a few.

All of us animals have a way of looking at events called an attitude. We get one from someone else and then keep it for our own for life whether it works for us or not. What makes it even more confusing is that any animal can have any attitude and use it freely whether it negates the really basic function of a particular animal's being or not.

THE BEGGING ATTITUDE   This one wants a little piece of what you have with the full knowledge that if she gets a little piece of what everyone she comes in contact with has, she will have about ten times more than anyone at the end of any particular day; this is not limited to objects, money or business deals—food works this way, too.

THE TEARING ATTITUDE   This one puts you off before you've finished your first sentence because the important thing about it is how she feels about whatever rather than several other possible considerations; it is critical for her to get this across as quickly as possible in order for her to beat the subject to the punch, so to speak, and so a few sniffles may be heard <u>before</u> anyone has said anything at all. Curious, isn't it—tears can demolish *any* sparring exercise no matter how pleased at the moment the other party may feel about how well everything is going.

THE TEASING ATTITUDE   This doesn't work until it is discovered what you hold important, and then it can work.

THE FORBIDDING ATTITUDE combines the best of what is forbidden with the formidable; don't ask, the answer is no! just as you open your mouth.

THE SMILING ATTITUDE   Whatever happens seems to be for the best if the smile is to be taken literally and it is so rare, it is inevitably taken literally.

All of these attitudes and MOs hang in a closet like so many wigs and costumes. We have only to choose and they are ours for the wearing. The mind behind the selection is bored and provides this first step of protection for us to get through our first day alive.

To the everlasting shock of the mind, however, most of us facing the next day from scratch, go right back to the same disguise we wore yesterday because of familiarity alone.

Whereas the mind only originally made a suggestion to get things started.

Old William was only half right: all the world is a stage, but the people on it are not all actors, actors know the advantage of changing their wig and costumes from time to time.

"Quiet, please. We have a motion on the floor to approve the minutes of our last meeting. Is there a second?"

SOLAR QUEANE

Margaret, her frail beauty belying an unflappable resolve, tended these days to listen more respectfully to those who would comment on her likeness to Jacqueline Bisset, now that she had quietly slipped past the half century mark. But unlike Ms. Bisset, whose expertise lay in persuasive characterizations embedded within a two-hour span, Margaret, as executive editor of her own magazine creation, Moment, knew something about long-term staying power, enjoyed perfecting what it took and, like an Olympic figure skater, excelled in what passed for seeming effortlessness.

She had never married, preferring to devote her energies to her publication over the years. This did not mean she was without relationships. On the contrary, she seemed to be in a particular one all the time. But each had been troubled, nervous, uneasy, short-lived—her need for perfection never finding male targets that could take it for long. At this time, she was without any particular companion, the last one who had lasted nearly three years, ended not with a bang or a whimper, an entity that simply atrophied out of her reality. She had busied herself redecorating her apartment, but after several weeks of repainting, recovering and redraping, she was bored and welcomed the call from Benner, eagerly responding to his suggestion to get together, surprised and delighted to hear his voice as strong as ever after more years than she wanted to count since they had seen each other.

They both chose the veal, a specialty at this intimate Italian restaurant where they had agreed to meet on Manhattan's east side. He drank off most of his Perrier and ordered another; she sensually toyed with a piece of endive between her teeth, basking in the comfort of their friendship.

"So, what's up?" she smiled at him.

"What do you mean? I just had an irresistible urge to see you again, that's all, Margaret, nothing more, really."

"Schorjak, unless they have lobotomized you and thrown away the parts, you never did anything disconnected from anything."

"True…so?"

"So, my old friend, what's up?" The largely untouched endive salad was deftly replaced by goose liver paté and a basket of crunchy fresh breads.

"Well, as long as you put it that way, Margaret…"

"Yeees…?"

"How long since you worked in legends, Margaret?"

Benner was referring to Margaret Leroux's earliest recognition as a writer, a young French authoress, heralded as carrying on tradition first established by Nathalie Sarraute, among other outspoken, gifted feminist intellectuals in the *avant garde* of their moment, her most provocative writing embedded in thinly disguised contemporary fairy tales.

"Goodness, years, I guess, except for a piece now and then, I have let the magazine completely consume my time. Why?"

Benner let out a long breath. The veal had arrived along with pasta and a thimbleful of what looked like eggplant and tomatoes.

"Tell me about legends. About why they exist, what their traditional function has been."

Margaret sipped her wine and sat back. "Well, legends come first. Few understand that aspect. We think of legends as something that were always there, emerging first in the dim, distant past. When they "work," they last, so most of the time they are thought of as legends of antiquity. But legends actually create the possibilities for action to follow, a guide, a psychological map and, of course, the necessary permission for the action to unfold, the necessary acceptability."

"Give me an example."

"Take contemporary fears of a population: a legend turns fears into dragons to be dispensed with through the courage of individuals. All the extensions of an era were given names, costumes, a narrative and some sort of denouement. They were not simply entertainment but dreams brought forward from the dark side, taken on as real by adventurers and explorers, who then pursued them in daylight."

"The dragonslayer." Benner motioned the waiter for coffee.

"Espresso?" the waiter asked, clearing the remaining dishes.

Margaret nodded. "Two," Benner said. He shifted his position and studied his friend. Everything she said counted. He listened intently, not wanting to miss or confuse anything she was telling him.

"Exactly," Margaret went on. "When a group of people get stuck on a problem, the collective imagination, what we think of as a critical mass, focuses on the problem and it has a tendency to get bigger, more detailed, more complex, expanding each day. We need legends and myths that create fresh perspectives, new paths to pursue or a problem can get to be dragon-size and, in some cases, destroy everything and everyone before it's done."

"That's what I want to hear next. What about today, tomorrow?"

"Simple: if the Little Tailor came over the mountains at great risk to himself to sew the hole in the sky through which the water kept pouring down on a kingdom getting drowned, then we need a little tailor to get up there and sew up the hole (at least find out for us if the hole presents any danger) in the ozone layer; we need a dragon slayer to destroy the pollution monsters and bring back clear skies—not just any monster but one that thrives on toxic poisons, comes to rest temporarily at the edge of a large, any large metropolitan city, welcoming the opportunity to sit down to a really substantial meal from week to week; in short we need new ways of thinking about everything so that it will be dealt with by each of us. Otherwise, bad things unattended to are apt to only get worse."

She folded her napkin. "Bigger than life, more courageous than man, more beautiful than woman, more outrageous than our problems, these are the stories that must come forward now."

"Star Wars?"

"A beginning. Look at the following for Star Trek! You see, if we are to have a space station, we need stories taking place on the space station for children every night. If we want to explore our own system, the same holds true. If we want toxic waste cleaned up, we need an intrepid adventurer or two who solves the toxic situations as an advanced detective, rising to the challenge rather than fleeing from the problem. Toxic Tamer, Have Card, Will Travel. Could be an exciting TV series."

"So, you're saying answers lie in our imagination, right?"

"As they always have." Margaret looked at her wristwatch. "I must go. Sadly enough, I need to go back to the office tonight. I have really enjoyed seeing you again, Benner."

On the street corner in front of her building, Benner held her arm.

"Think about the media, Margaret. I love everything you say. But your media, the print industry, is holding us back."

"No question about its limitations."

"No, more than limitations, those new perspectives you mentioned, couldn't we explore colors, sounds, perhaps integrated with some traditional text, to expand language?"

"I get the feeling you are not saying something here."

"There is an entity, defying description, lying off of our orbit but moving perceptibly, almost regally."

"Is that all that's known?"

"There's more, much more, but it can keep for now. Leave it that it is a completely unknown phenomena and that alone could cause panic, could cause havoc. We need an explanation before we are able to provide one, is what it amounts to."

"How much time do we have, Benner?"

"Very little."

"You were talking about a legend. What is creating the need for one, for a legend?"

"We have been aware for some time that a dark star has moved in behind our sun. It won't stay there permanently. When it comes round, if it continues to transit toward our orbit...I understand there is a massive focus on defense strategies going on in the military sector, from nuclear to a list of fission technologies being designed to thwart this object, big enough to end life on this planet as we know it."

"Really?"

"Hmm, at any rate, that's it, that's what the legend needs to help explain. Meanwhile, we are doing everything we can to try to control its path."

"A legend of that sort today is called a cover story, Benner."

"I guess."

"And specifically, the cover story needs to…?

"…help avoid hysteria from sweeping the globe once this dark star becomes visible?"

"I see."

"Will you take it on?"

"I'll see what I can come up with."

They hugged lightly, exchanged kisses on the cheek and parted.

Late that night, Margaret stood by her bedroom window looking out across the city toward the East, toward the spot on the horizon where the sun rose every morning.

"But why should we always be fearful every time we deal with the unknown," she thought.

She carried her laptop over to the bed, pulled the covers back, crawled in and slid the computer on to her lap.

Once upon a time," she typed, *"a dark star picked its way across the universe until it reached our galaxy. It paused there, behind our sun, unsure about which way to go around because it was a very large, very hot and very violent sun. Astronomers, who had been tracking this star for several years, were alarmed because to them it looked like it had chosen to attempt to hide there out of sight. Which way it turned at that point was of secondary concern to this star because, above all else, it knew it was home.*

Margaret paused to plump up her pillows a bit, then settled back, gazed out the window for a moment and continued her typing.

It had no way of knowing what kind of systemic welcome it would receive. It was unknown, unexpected, and very late in arriving. The other planets had all settled in quite awhile back. Further, it knew that the unknown, the unexpected, and the late arrival could possibly not be welcomed at all. In fact, it might meet with an uncontrolled fear that could spread throughout the system and, in the end, bring harm to the star itself. It was not altogether ignorant of fear, it had had a few starts itself as it was moving across the universe. Not everything that's out there has been explained as yet. By any means.

Scientists have discovered a star of multi-colors that is emerging from behind the sun.

She could see the headlines. In fact, she would run this story in Moment in place of her usual editorial. What had Benner said, "sounds, too?"
She picked up the thought.

The announcement went on to say that by listening with giant receptors over a period of weeks, every once in awhile a pattern of tones could be distinguished above the radio noise. The presidential Commission for the Analysis of New Astral Objects (ANAO) could go no further for the time being.

But the star was moving again. Already visible,
its changing hues of blue and green, dark orange and
reds create a fascinating night sky pageant.

Margaret wondered what might cause it to resist
gravitational pulls as it passes other bodies, not to mention black holes, million-mile-an-hour stellar winds,
swirling gaseous starmaking centers, without diverting its
course in the slightest? And how many light years must it
have traveled by now, unswerving in its mission to what?
Return, like a monarch long in exile, returning to its
rightful place, a queen returning to her own court…(in
deference to the elapsed time, Margaret chose the ar-
chaic spelling Queane).

She reverted to the historical perspective and went on.

It grew in size each day. Would it resist our
planet's gravitational field, as well? She corrected
that to read: Of course, as it turned out, it resisted
our planet's gravitational field, as well.

Then Margaret relaxed, smiling inwardly, knowing
that the legend Benner needed was emerging.

If there was any underlying navigational scheme,
it would be that it had been moving from sun to sun
in a restless search, a strangely disturbing but
captivating entity, like a proud, homecoming
medieval queane, a solar queane, generating her own
mysterious light, her own musical language, floating
out there in the distance through the trees.

OUTWARD BOUND

It was amazing for me the other day to realize that nudity one hundred years ago was pretty much like it is today. This revelation took place while perusing a collection of tinted photos of early sailing ships. Yearning but unable to be OUTWARD BOUND as the book was called, I was startled, on turning the page, by a bevy of swim-suited bathing beauties smiling, posturing, waving and beckoning to the reader from their New England seaside location. Having been studying and comparing the bow and transom, sheer and tumblehome, loftiness and rake of each preceding ship, I looked similarly at those females who had so suddenly appeared, with the same eye for diameter of waist, length of leg, curve of hip, abundance of breast, set of shoulder, and expression of eye. And with their dark stockings rolled part-way down and their under-shorts and skirts falling above, the one area that really catches the eye is that of the nude knee.

The knees of these ladies do not quite have an expression but they do have an attitude probably derived from what they've had to do so far, how they've had to do it, and how much weight they've carried while accomplishing it. Some knees are coyly dimpled, some are downright strong, some are bony, some are not, and some are simply nondescript with an air of indifference as if they just happened to be where they were but were not involved in any way. The bathing costumes are dated as are the hair styles, but the naked knees are quite the same phenomena you would find today were you to visit a public bathing area just to see for yourself.

There was a moment when the potential of the inner-face of the knees and their attitudes might have been brought to the attention of the American Public. Artists such as Jasper Johns and Larry Rivers were repainting the American flag, Campbell soup cans and labels were represented exactly, and a gym class of underwear-clad males and females appeared at one point, their self-consciousness of body frailties highlighting the expression of the mural. And there were the knees, pairs and pairs of them. It is a wonderful study but, being half-naked, the facial expressions take over above those of the inner-faces of the knees. And so the gambit is lost until, at last, I am able to bring it forward on these pages.

And here it is. Looking closely, again I observed that, to my astonishment, there seemed to be seven types of basic knees, accompanied, of course, by their respective attitudes.

I am happy that this all fits in so well with where we are today. It is obvious from the tens of thousands of inspirational publications we Americans purchase monthly, each of which carry their respective message in the form of two or four or six or eight or ten principles, commandments, tenets, thou shalts or try-to's, directed at redeeming our health, spirit, weight, career, marriage, or credit, that we are a nation that eagerly responds to a few simple whatevers. Not too many, not too few—but just the right amount to easily remember during the course of the day that we may not flounder into unprincipled helplessness on our own. And now I have my own, seven in number, basic and categorized, a simple guide to the higher order of everything.

As a juvenile male, I cannot remember being too interested in the knee patterning of my own male peers. But I can tell you about several young female variables of the seven basic matures, *i.e.,* knees with attitude.

There was, for example, Sonia Iberg, who was six when I was six, and who during recess would smile and wave at me across the playground, and if I didn't respond, would plant a penny wrapped in a scrap of bubble gum wrapper on my desk when we raced back into our classroom, had small, incredibly strong red/white knees that allowed her to run faster than a speeding baseball when she wanted to.

Or there was Jeanne Falouffe, who was five when I was five, and who brought for her favorite personal item to a show-and-tell morning, a pert frog in a shoebox, whose name was William, she sweetly proclaimed, who loved her dearly and she him, whose dimpled inner-faces were formed like steam holes in a cheese-covered casserole.

Then there was Doris Hornsby, who dragged me enthusiastically to the back of the auditorium during a tediously lengthy school play rehearsal when she was nine and I was nine, turning excitedly into the last row of seats, plumping us down, fixing me with a STARE OF PROMISE while pulling up her skirt and right panty-leg to reveal her appendicitis scar, who had a knee arrangement perpetually upraised in a Groucho Marx eyebrow wiggle.

And not to mention Miriam Swearingen, who miraculously went from a frog, when we were both seven, to a swan at nine and back to a frog at eleven, who had patellas sublimely indifferent to knee action functions.

I think of the Levinson sisters, whose background included lots of money, arriving as they did each morning in a long black limousine, had truly virgin inner-faces, for in seven years I never once had a glimpse of their knees, covered as they were summer, spring, fall and winter, with long stockings of various shades under long skirts.

And Jackie May Elgin, who had more muscle in her left upper arm than the whole after-school fifth grade two-hand touch football team put together, whose knees rippled and cross-rippled with energy reserves.

Or Barbara Trilling, ah yes, dear Barbara, on whose team we fought to be on rainy-day indoor dodgeball efforts, whose knees, like her lovely little face, and hands, and blond curly hair, and small compact figure, were as near-perfect an inner-face as I was ever to know—on or off the dodgeball courts of later years.

But already we are discussing here forms of hybrids, variations, crossbreeding of the seven basic matures. It takes far more than one lifetime to get to know and recognize the infinite possibilities. How few of us know our own inner-face before it is too late. Which is to say that the best analysis should take place standing in your bathroom sink and observing in your medicine cabinet mirror your own set of knees before you are thirty-six inches tall. The second best way, and it can only be an approximation, to sense what the inner-face expression on your knees may be, is to concentrate on them with closed eyes in a relaxed sitting position. The feeling you should have if you make contact is like a tingling sensation without the tingle.

The first time this happened to me, I cannot erase from memory, nor want to. It was near the end of the seventh year of dabbling in the aura of Ah-yes-Barbara that our bare arms briefly touched one afternoon as we were shoving them through the playground fence at Mr. Gazzini, the water ice man. For two cents he would squirt syrup on a cup of ice scraped from a never diminishing block of ice.

"Root beer!" I shouted, finally gaining the front of the little crowd up against the fence.

"Cherry!" the near-perfect inner-face sang out next to me as our arms touched waving fists that held the pennies. For three cents you got extra squirts. And it was worth it. If you held the paper cup of flavored crushed ice of a three-center a couple of minutes in your fist, the melting liquid surged to the top and that first sip, with your nose in the crushed ice and the root beer, in my case, spilling down a parched throat on a warm spring afternoon in May, lists as one of those few incomparable experiences that this short life might disclose to the fortunate chosen. It could be topped, however, and was, as my gaze lifted to lock in on Ah-yes-Barbara's sparkling blue eyes just ten inches from mine, whose own parchedness was at that very moment being relieved by the veritable flooding of icy cherry liquids rushing to meet their responsibilities. It was in that moment of cherry/root beer floodtide intimacy that a sensation filled my entire being that can best be thought of as an incredible tingling but with the tingle!

The advantage of wearing pants that cover the knees as against skirts that don't quite is that once covered, knees quickly lose their self-consciousness and begin to probe around. Something like flicking on the road lights mounted on a roll bar above the cab of a pickup truck, they discern the indiscernible, assimilate the unassimilatable, and deliver all to the patient and politely bored brain center for careful analysis. Pants- covered knees do very well under a table around which are seated females with uncovered knees staring helplessly straight ahead.

One midmorning in fall on the upper east side of Manhattan, I found myself in just exactly that position. Eight of us, seated around a small directors' table, were completing the interview process that had been going on for weeks that would ultimately approve my being selected as a consultant for an arts support group of nationwide dimensions. National New Audiences felt that the nation's cultural consciousness badly needed raising and they, National New Audiences, needed, therefore, to be doing just that.

Or rather, a few members of the national board, largely living within walking distance of the offices on upper Park Avenue, felt good about feeling they needed to be doing just that. As long as they didn't have to travel out there to any of those—distant cities—where the various chapters of the organization thrived or disintegrated each season. Hence the use of consultants. Traveling consultants in the arts of the nation! Like flying ants sent out to teach everyone how to be fireflies.

Mary Anne, who knew she was the most important person in the room, simply, if not only, because her European mother was the most important person in the arts (of Europe), cleared her throat and said from her end of the table, "Well, I'd like to know exactly why Richard…" she flicked through her file copy of my papers, "uh, oh, Quanta really wants to join our little family."

Didi, at Mary Ellen's left, leaned forward out of her mink wrapping—she had one for each week of the New York winter season—and proffered, "I think we should hear from him about that in his own words," quickly withdrawing into the dead animal kingdom with which she was so accustomed to surrounding herself.

Across the table, Beverly, whose tanned and lean body could now only start a shrinking process from the relentless effort of youthening—dieting, jogging, tennising, steaming, dry heating, massaging—she put herself through daily, volunteered, "Girls, I just flew in from Denver where my daughter and son-in-law have opened this darling soup and salad restaurant with butcher-block tables and checkered table cloths and are doing extraordinarily well when you think they have been open such a short while and with so little backing to start with, so I have not had time to read," thumbing quickly through her file copy of papers, "uh, about, uh, Mr. Cantu..."

"Quanta," a correcting chorus proffered.

"Right, Mr. Quanta, but I tend to agree with Didi."

"About what?" asked James B. Downing, the Executive Director. James B., as he preferred to be recognized, was a small person who tended toward the edge of any chair he sat in because his upper legs bent too soon to sit all the way back.

"About restaurants, I presume," murmured Gene Reston, National Program Director, a hopeful Hugh Hefner philosopher of the organization, who had recently added a pipe to his bell-bottom jeans and tweed jacket ensemble, and who was right now subtly underlying his remark by knocking his dead pipe against the heel of a black shoe. Gene, like Hugh and the Palomar telescope, had flurries with life each evening and, with each sortie, gained additional information that only added to his existing uncertainties. For ten years and more, Reston had experienced a bewildering succession of disaster-ridden female relationships, the blatant fact of which had never hooked up in his perception for helps or insights into each new adventure. Hence, the gradual adoption of a philosophical pose, one can only assume, no thanks to the knees.

"About what, Beverly?" repeated James B, thinly disguising his impatience over the interruptive aside. James B. treated interruptions in the same manner a CPA treats moral protestations for accounting errors. Someone told me years later, trying to provide a reasoning for tolerance, I suppose, that James B. had been raised by five maiden aunts. In Baltimore.

Quiet until now, but always driven by a restless sense of guilt if not being able to make a significant policy contribution, Billie Vandergriffen, brushed busily at something only she could see clinging to the lapel of her tailored navy suit.

"We're losing the thread here," June Billingsly interjected, preoccupied with Billie's actions. "I think," she went on, her dark hair framing a pageboy's face, "Mary Ellen's question has the floor and then I have one of my own."

"I'd like to point out at this point," Gene headed toward commas to suck his pipe alight, "that the concept here, the concept in mind when I recommended my good friend Richard here, (hsp), the concept we should all keep in front of us during this next period, the uh several important and, I must remind you, overriding concerns, in addition, James B., to your responsibilities with the short and long-range financial structuring, (hsp), (hsp)..." James B. winced at the mention by Program staff of any responsibilities of his own; he let them alone, whatever it was they were supposed to be doing, and he only asked as Executive Director, for similar treatment.

"...(hsp) (hsp)...including curricular considerations might be the best way to bring to this dialogue, this discussion—" Gene was off down his own backstretch to his unique technique of philopsychologizing.

My under-the-table sensors were vibrating with communication still, focused, as they were, on June. Could she be related to the Billingsly's of the Billingsly Foundation?

The Billingsly Foundation, as listed, I had once called for their guidelines on non-profit grant funding only to be put in touch with a sweet young voice who said, "Foundations, may I help you?"

"Foundations?" I had repeated uncertainly.

"Yes, sir, what can I do for you this morning?"

"Well, I uh need to know your guidelines."

"Guidelines for what?"

"For what you do—?"

"I see. Well, this department covers just about everything you might need in foundations..."

"Oh, good."

"Hmmm? including girdles, half girdles, bras and panties, lingerie...what is your special interest this morning, sir?"

"Financing for a non-profit project," I mumbled.

"Oh? Let me transfer you to the operator, hello, hello, I really don't know why she gave you Ladies Undergarmentry in the first place...."

"(hsp)...the concept of introducing predetermined cut-off points, deadlines if you will, with sufficient lead time to permit the exercise of selective discrimination (hsp), a weeding process (hsp), (hsp), a type of quality control that is long overdue (hsp), (hsp), (hsp), and I feel strongly that Richard here, is just the person to accomplish this work with diplomacy, calm under crossfire, and all the while, never compromising the standards we must enforce on behalf of our national organization's responsibility to the arts of this country." The long-dead pipe had started up and Gene now began quietly coughing.

"Uh, Mr. Quanta," Katie, the lint having been removed finally, was making her move, putting a little question in, just for the record of this meeting, "tell us, if you can, just what kind of experience, or rather, just what there is in your background that makes you feel that you can handle this kind of responsibility? It is, after all, dealing with children, people, large funds, long distances, you see." She fluttered a self-appreciative glance around the table.

"What kind of responsibility?" Beverly looked up from her first read-through of the file everyone else had perused by now.

"Well, you know, the one Gene just described. In my experience, the first and last thing we want to remember is the importance of substance, of substantial responsibility in whatever we're trying to do here. I remember, for example..." Katie was about to launch into references to her one cultural program experience, something she was want to bring up two or three times a meeting, something that had taken place over two decades earlier, something called "Cultural Reconstruction" paid for with funds she had personally gleaned from the city through the then Mayor of New York, a program, in short, which provided all the prisoner inmates of Rikers Island with a free instrument, a paid-for symphonic instrument, which was to provide the prisoners with a sense-of-being-a-part-of-the-finer-things-in-life, and which, however, provided them with pocket money as soon as they were able to liberate these instruments and sell them to the nearest available broker, bringing the reconstruction of said prisoners to a rapid and final and, some said, somewhat scandalous end. Forever.

"We have a question on the floor," Didi hurriedly put in before Billie had her teeth too firmly set on the next thirty minutes.

"I believe Mary Ellen asked that…"

"I can speak for myself quite nicely, thank you, Didi," Mary Ellen bristled, "and that is all I am asking Mr. Quanta to do."

My probe sensors were quiet again, roaming. "I was wondering," I began, smiling graciously, "if you are related in any way, Mrs. Billingsly, to the Billingsly Foundation?" I did not mean to ignore Mary Ellen, whom I knew the importance of, but I felt it was a good diplomatic ploy to divert authority right off and make the lesser members shine.

"It is in my husband's corporation, yes, why do you ask?"

"Well, I was just sitting here recalling an incident that once happened to me that would amuse you, all of you, I'm sure," I went on, relaxing, with the control of the whole group in my hands. One simply gets to know when everything is going so well that you cannot possibly make a mistake.

"I was once charged with the mission of finding funds for a publication, an arts publication, a non-commercial arts publication, of course, and in the process found myself calling the Billingsly offices," June nodded, "and was given the Ladies Garmentry Department instead." I was chuckling now over the richness of the incident.

"Apparently, I had been connected with the Department Store of the same name." I was aware that no one else was chuckling. "Foundations…you know, girdles, panties, bras…"

There are some silences that fall upon us so perfect, so complete, that they must be meant for extra-terrestrial journey else they would be wasted.

James B. was the first to pull the rug over that particular black hole.

"Ladies, it is time for me to ring that little annoying mental bell for all of you and say that it is one minute after twelve, this room has been reserved by my staff who have been excused from lunch in order to stuff folders for the Finance Committee meeting that is to start promptly at 12:45. Your lunch has been prepared in the reception room, and may I remind you that we are greeting the President and two board members of the San Francisco Chapter at 2:45 in my office. I think we can say that this has been a productive and entirely worthwhile session altogether and I would like to thank all of you, along with Mr. Quanta, of course, for joining us this morning."

Everyone quickly rose. In time, I, too, was to learn the trick of injecting the sense-of-purpose-having-been-intelligently-furthered bringing needed satisfaction to everyone—and great relief at being able to close a meeting neatly avoiding any action required.

And there it was. The women, whose uncovered inner-faces would have betrayed them before they could speak, had learned the importance of sitting around a directors' table whenever conducting business that needed a seriousness not otherwise readily available to them. The men (staff) soon learned to check their sense of humor, along with any other dangerous weapons, at the door before entering into any foray specifically concerning the Arts of This Nation.

The explorer follows winding roads because, like mountains for the climber, first of all, they are there, but secondly, to see where they lead, and only down through the years does the third element emerge, intrigued as he becomes with what happens should they run out.

I wondered, at that time, if the concept of the inner-face, as revealed to me so far by naked knees, could be applied to cities. If I was given the opportunity to get to know the energizing components—economics, politics, education, health, industry, law enforcement—a first-hand view of how these components were converted for human use, a view through the window of the arts, a sort of knee-level perspective, could there possibly be revealed an inner-face of a city?

The sense of theatre, abundant in some male Taureans lying near the Ariesian border, coupled as it is with a restless urge for adventure, seeks the company of an attractive female, shortly before departure time, with whom he can enjoy the ineluctable agonies of saying goodbye.

During the first several weeks of my employment, largely spent at the national offices being oriented and perusing endless files, I was brought up short one morning just as I passed an office around the corner from Gene's, when papers slid quickly out of control through the open doorway to scatter on the floor.

"Oh dear!" exclaimed a voice from inside. I instinctively kneeled to begin gathering up some of the pages when I found myself looking into a pair of near-perfect knees!

I stood up immediately about to say, "My God, ah-yes-Barbara, what is a girl like you doing in a place like this?" when the same voice I'd just heard now said, "Hi, excuse the mess, I'm Pru." The outstretched hand, the beautiful smile, the pretty face, the long loose well-coiffed tresses had me held instant prisoner. She was more than could ever be hoped for as a, miracle of miracles, near-perfect goodbye girl!

I mentally dabbled in Pru's aura for the next little while and began to hope that I wouldn't be having to stay out on the road too long for my first go'round. I found reasons to stop by her office often. She was bright, and pretty, and always well groomed, loved to laugh, and seemed to be involved in a dozen things at once. A high order Gemini, as she once called herself, had entered my life. When she had to go to Philadelphia on business for the national office, I found reasons to accompany her on the train returning late in the afternoon that same day.

"What for?" queried Gene.

"It will help my indoctrination," I explained. He reluctantly approved my expenses, adding, "Just don't mention this to James B. for the time being, OK?"

That day in Philadelphia slipped by in business consultations, luncheon, even a peek in at a fundraising fashion show. We stood together on the 30th street station deck waiting for the commuter to train us back to Manhattan.

"The Philadelphia Chapter has some rather complicated aspects to its history," Pru said, the wind blowing her hair lightly across her face.

"So do I," I thought to myself.

"You are going to find these distinctions, special considerations, with just about every situation you'll be working with across the country."

I thought about bare arms touching through a schoolyard fence, root beer racing down my throat, thought about never returning to New York if I could persuade her to cross with me to the opposite platform and catch the train to somewhere else together, right then.

"Once you leave New York," she went on, "the arts become much more than performances, paychecks, bookings, management—as Gene and James B. tend to define things. They become intertwined with the community and each place has its own way of handling organizations."

(No chance, I guess. Well, if not forever, how about staying on in Philadelphia for a couple of days?)

We caught a cab in New York and I got out to let her out on 57th street in front of Carnegie Hall. I was absorbed watching the near-perfect knees slide out first.

"Thanks for the lift," she touched my arm lightly, "see you at the office tomorrow," and she was gone in the sidewalk crowd before I could answer.

One morning soon after, I sought Pru out to begin my ineluctable goodbye strategy as in just one week I had been told I would be venturing forth. I found her in her office—packing.

"Hey, you can't leave now!" I cried.

She looked up and then smiled at me as if reading ulterior thoughts were as easy as watching my face.

"Well, unfortunately…" she began but was interrupted.

Some people burst into rooms, others knock tentatively. James B. always reminded me of having been set down gently on the threshold for he seemed to slipper in.

"Pru, what is going on?" although the packing was self-evident.

"I'm leaving, as I'm sure you can see."

"I had no idea."

"I gave you a month's notice of my resignation."

"When?"

"Thirty days ago."

"I don't recall, I'm sorry, Pru, I wish I had known you were unhappy. I would have done something about it."

Pru's eyes rolled to the ceiling then she quickly refocused on her packing. James B. slippered out. All I could think was that my near-perfect goodbye girl was pulling out on me a week ahead of schedule, as far as I was concerned, and where was I going to find another one on such quick notice with her smile, quality, stature, mind and most importantly, her near-perfect knees?

But she was slipping away even as I thought these thoughts and I knew deep down that our knees would forever remain unknown to each other. There would never be that incredible moment of confrontation—inner-face to inner-face.

I know now, of course, that perfect or even near-perfect knees do not exist. Anywhere. Over time I came to realize that what I thought I glimpsed, the knees portraying a secret inner face, was simply carefully disguised character clues worn between chin and forehead, you know—disguised anguish, suppressed uncertainties, nostalgic longing, the who, in short, we really are, dressed in scratchy woolen bathing costumes, our stockings needing pulling up, our tight pants down, our flowery skirts arranged, our beach hats clutched in one hand, the other waving in cheery desperation, squinting at the invisible few, that oh-so-fortunate handful whose inner-faces have turned away from us, turned away to be stoically facing the future, turned away to be Outward Bound!

ESTUARIES

Poetry

BACK TO THE TIDES

Now that I have discovered sonnet form, I can include
the meanings found scattered through this life,

Meanings once divested from novel, opera, mural, delude
no more, their function done, as with a midwife.

What's left behind can easily fit in my sea bag, still
half empty, room yet for one more slender volume—
what does

one take when there are moments to decide—how to fill
a canvas sack—with what is…or was?

Or will be? I must save room for that bronze hammer, knife
and silver spurs, funny—he felt he had to have his axe
for Walden—strange thoughts to have while one packs

boots, heavy sweater, rough jacket, thick socks—one pair,
marlinspike and compass, this side pocket amply hides,
Soon I'll be homeward bound at last, back to the tides.

STASIS

The sky is blue and clear,
There is no cloud to mar it,

The land, well, the land is flat out here,
and not one tree to scar it.

And the sand is the sand of an ancient ocean,
without one drop remaining,

But five small colored stones at toes-end,
antiquity containing.

A glimpse of perfection
at arms-length, a collection
of a million years in stasis…

Now I look around again at four or five
of any nearest me alive,
and see the same perfection in their faces.

Terms

I have considered all there is to learn
and before my head fills with indifference

as its final defense, it is not to spurn
the already learned that I share this confidence.

An observation starts out like a minnow,
pleased and contented in a world which turns out to be
    the edge of an ocean,

From whence it soon seeks and ceaselessly acquires new
    facts to place in tow,
It thereby begets an open-ended system. So, like a
    whale in motion…

It now needs quantities of data for its maw,
as the whale, now full-grown, proceeds in endless quest,
for the million-plankton-mouthful knows no rest.

But one who carefully contains an observation within
    its own moment,
Proceeds to learn as much as can be uncovered,
The Universe on its own terms alone determining
    what shall be discovered.

November

These years hurrying toward some kind of cadence
at which point I hope there comes a pause

in this long acceleration turning months into days; since
I no longer think, my time obeys new laws.

Perceptual reformation seems to have its own
inexorable pathway, a course that leads

further inward toward the moment, a lone
proof of lifeforce' indifference to past deeds.

This gray November afternoon has its own strains
of contentment, the shorn corn stands
        my horse canters through,
black distant cattle dots, all this a watchful hawk maintains.

Once conscious of their passing, I give each moment title,
stretching out each day and night a little longer,
making my life the richer and so much more vital.

Five Mile Line

I drove into Mentone on Friday
to visit the Judge, but he'd gone.

Well, there's the Sheriff, boots, hat, gun, ok?
He nodded, stared, sought possible wrong.

"Mentone's a town with twenty-nine souls,
We ran outta water last year,

Trouble is we drilled plentya holes
but there's nothin' but oil around here."

Sounds easy, so six of us bid on a five-mile line,
Whoa now! Five of us got out just in time –
Low bidder beware, best take stock:

Contract calls to ditch and bury that old pipe,
but 'fore you're done prairie dust'll bring tears to wipe,
'cause there's nothing down there but haaaard rock.

THE MAGIC CLOSET STAFF

To whom it may concern: I hereby unequivocally state –
    these lines are not mine,
much as I'd like to weave some of them
    into my personal loom, at least try,

There are certain nomad members of this
    strange desert dream
who'll claim I lie.

A clue, they'll say, is that they're neat,
they have the proper iambic feet,

While mine seem to roam all over these West Texas plains,
like a transplanted Northeastern flower looking for rains.

So I dedicate this tome, like it or not,
to those who shaped this sonnet's plot,
But I will NOT print each name,

For why should Fleur-de-lis Strewnwell,
H.R. Stringer Fludd III, Tuscaloosa,
C. Capture Lemming, Tippykal, and the
Right Reverend Wm. Hosanna receive all the fame?

THE WEED

Hope sprouts like a weed looking for sunlight
    and a little rain –

if it finds both, the world of the weed
    is a mighty fine place to be –
it grows strong, flourishes and becomes a beautiful thing

For a weed is simply an unplanned baby –
given a chance, it has a right to be –
    just as any hothouse plant –

and because it does and will always walk on the wild side,
all other kinds of plant life benefit and are advantaged.

It brings the qualities to life so long exorcised
    from so many –
courage, independence, assertiveness, humor,
reflection, incredible adaptability –

all this because perhaps it realizes it is only a weed.
Which is a little like being on borrowed time –
it makes all effort precious,

and being rather pleased with its own survival,
it is good to be around, it exudes a joyous energy –

and for just being twice-blessed with sun and rain,
the world is now one weed removed
    from suffering and pain.

CHRONOS

The root in darkness forms a stem.
Rains fall, winds blow young leaves,
Sun—and the bloom is hastened,
within its own time, to become
...and the circle starts to spin.

Goodbye to yesterday
the wind has blown it away
The rain has melted the snow on the ground
and I feel like a ride on the merry go round.
And I feel like a ride on the merry go merry go round.

I hear someone calling I know
But I have some place to go,
The pretty horses all dance on the rim
And it seems like the earth is beginning to spin,
And it seems like the earth is beginning, beginning to spin.

The geese fly north through the sky
But I can catch up if I try
For I have a horse with a golden mane
And we're going to gallop away just the same,
And we're going to gallop away.
Singing goodbye to yesterday,
Singing goodbye, singing goodbye to yesterday.

And so I become and grow and bend and discover
I can feel, and think, and know…
Summer is a time that lasts forever
I will find a name in late September
Now is a balloon tugging at its tether
No one else can know what I'll remember…when…
And so I become, and wonder at my life,
and wander with my life.

Summer is a time that lasts forever
I will find a name in late September.

Not for me the dreams of life spent dreaming
broken cymbal graves with faded ribbons streaming,

leave the shallow sculptured places
turn from smiling tearless faces

early Autumn spins the circle…
brilliant colors everywhere are falling

deep within the spectrum geese are calling
fragments of an icy wind that's blowing

follow me and follow knowing
winter dreams all flow together in the Spring
within my own time, my own time.

Until night falls,

and I feel again
IN DARKNESS

*(Singing
goodbye to
yesterday…*

as I once was,
THE ROOT

*the wind has
blown it away.)*

rooted, in earth
FORMS

beneath the stars,
ALONE.

SOMETHING PERFECT

Life forms by fertilizing inarticulate feelings with thought.
If the *feelings* are not there, the result is not truly one's own
　　potential form.
If the *thought* does not take place, the urge
　　subsides inchoate,
　　locked into its early stages of formation.
The observation is that human development
　　does not happen naturally in successive stages,
But over and over again embryonically,
　　many times short-lived, only sometimes fully realized.
It is often choked off when we look around
　　to see what's going on
and then attempt to join in whether it is for us or not.

When the impulse to act is caused by external sources,
　　there is little likelihood that it will result
　　in one's own life form.

Life forms and dissolves lightly like clouds.

When we attempt to hold on to a dissolving form
    or force a forming one,
The effort produces results that are not what we hoped
    and which usually require great amounts
    of physical energy to maintain.
The flow is missing.

Life-forms do not have time lines.
Whether several seconds or several years are involved
    depends only on our understanding
        of what is going on.

Heed the inarticulate urge or deeply felt desire.
Let life form around it.
Let it go if it does not develop.
You will keep forming and reforming until
    something perfect happens.

THE OTHERS

She started out with a clean slate
and looked a lot and listened some and then
                    did something.
Which the others considered to be the result of
                    _____ PERCEPTION!

And, as it usually turned out to be ok,
she responded to everything new –
                    the same way.
And the others referred to it as_____ TECHNIQUE!

When she headed into subsequent situations,
it polished her technique –
                    to a high level!
Those same people—the others— named it _____ VISION!

So now, with a little help from ordinary time,
a life story, her own narrative –
                    has been created!
Which, of course, the others call _____ DESTINY!

But in all confidence, she told me the other day
that if she could stop becoming what she dreamed –
               and start over with a clean slate –
She would be happy to turn in PERCEPTION,
                 TECHNIQUE,
               STYLE,
             VISION &
            DESTINY from now on for…
– if the others have to call it something –
        let them call it,
            (she said to me, lowering her voice),
            let them call it – you know,
            just being.

THE INVISIBLES

She simply appeared one night while I was sleeping, woke
me gently, sat down on the edge of the bed in her own soft
radiance and spoke briefly in a low but vibrant voice.

"Let us call particular aspects of the human species
        The Invisibles," she said.
"Everyone is aware of them, no one has ever seen them.
They are bundled within the human spirit.
This spirit world of invisible attributes is the
        connective link of life.

Of the several billion manifestations of this spirit, the
human body, none are alike. But the invisibles are similar
and with their like energies, run freely throughout the
human kingdom.

The body is like a scoop of clay into which flow
        the invisibles.
When the body wears out, the invisibles flow back into a sea
        of spirit, depthless and endless.

The spirit sea is what makes you possible.
As long as it is there, you will continue to exist as a species.

The invisibles permeate all.
Walls do not keep them out, walls do not keep them in.
Walls only restrain bodies which are a temporary pinchup
        of sand and water.
When the invisibles depart,
        the body dissolves into sand and water again."

There was a beat of silence.
She leaned over my head and whispered,
"Do not listen to the words of the dwellers of caves
but follow the songs of the wind and the sea."

And she was gone.

AQUITANE

In the end,
there is no one time
as against another.

All time
and all concepts of time,
though grand or groveling,
disposed toward chivalry
or reveling in brutality,
whether starseeking effort
or noselength acquisition,
All concepts become defined
by each novitiate
who would forge a link
in the endless spiraling circuitry
of human existence.

Time simply measures;
It is we who choose,

But that measurement
is the scale of our humanity.

For one, a battle to be faced at dawn,
for another, the first contact
with the fantasy of love,
and for a third,
the closing gap of failing memory.

Thus we weave ourselves
into each other's history,
and thus I
would weave you into mine.

STEADY STATE

Focusing without thought

Using instead of owning

Listening for direction

Discovering the moment.

Acting surely on swift impulse

Knowing in place of seeing

Returning all at end of day

Entering the moment.

THE CROSSING

Follow me and we will find all the sun strewn days ahead,
follow me and we will find a strawberry field for our bed,
    where you can rest your head,
    where you can rest your head.

Come and see the leaves turn once again,
come with me and walk again the pathways followed,
winds softly sigh,
    pathways followed as a child.

In the evening chill,
    hear the shouts and calls of friends,
    friends played with
    just beyond the hill.

Shadows start to lengthen,
cries, cries of distant birds now winging home,

Here begins a different time,
    time for us alone.
Come take my hand
    and we will start *our* journey home.

STILLIFE

Story Theater

Fourteen Cinemagrams

A very beautiful woman of passion, intellect and spirit, brushes her hair seated in front of a large mirror frame through which she faces the audience. It is late afternoon. She must arrange last minute details for a dinner party she has planned for the evening. Sometime earlier that day, she has received a note of regret from the man with whom she has had a lengthy and uneven relationship. She is speaking her thoughts and we are provided scenes of her mind's eye running back over her lifetime taking place, however, during a passing moment of that afternoon. This script is a sequence of cinematographic segments or cinemagrams, interior thought locations explored in the woman's contemplation.

The mind rarely takes a singular path, bringing in connections and associations as it sees appropriate to build the mosaic of the filmic mural. The camera moves freely in the same manner.

1. Setting The Act

WOMAN:
> I think, perhaps, it's…imagery –
> bereft of silences, some space, a little time –
> cannot take place.
> It *has* no place.

> These sounds, my words, some color,
> or a sculpted piece of bronze,
> must each first find silence, space, and time,
> designed compatibly.

> An outline of desire.
> To consequently *come to life.*
> And so there is this one regard:
> That once some spatial silence
> receives its own dimensioned time,
> that act is set.

> The object now exists by virtue of its confines.
> No more, no less.

> A curious thought has just begun…
> Do I…exist within these castled sands
> by virtue of the walls around me?
> Do I, preparing for this evening's guests,
> spend time that's mine?

> Or is the premonition, with which I rose
> this dawn, of death…my truth?

2. PERSPECTIVE SHIFT

(Brief break while she moves restlessly about, then returns to seated position. Change of lighting tone accompanies this break.)

WOMAN:

I wonder if, within these towered walls,
there lies some other truth for me,
whose lies are only partially submerged by casual
reflection.

Why my life *appears* to me to be constricting,
on the verge of closure,
would place the total burden on appearance.

And this seems neither logical nor even
fair...although,
I know, that what *'appears'* *'to be'*
is not contrived of logic,
and occurs quite easily
beyond the realm of all—that's fair.

Can this be the moment madness starts?
For suddenly, all things become an apparition,
and there is more and more within, within,
within –
So little time is left to see...
when everything is brilliantly so beautiful...

Reflections cast reflections—through my own
      mirror
I can see the premonition growing....

Dark...drop...blown....
Chaste moon, dartlight glisten,
dance reflecting, run raced –

Bleak autumnal tomb,
chasing broken scarlet shadows,
gazing lifelessly....

3. VISITORS

(The woman now moves in a more limited area of proscenium stage. The MAN and The SECOND WOMAN are eventually seen on either side of forestage.)

WOMAN:
Where is my pen?
If I've so little time to try to tie together
all that's hanging....
I must answer him.
Where is my pen?
His letter...*(studies it)*

MAN: *(burst of laughter in darkness as she is reading the letter – then spot light slowly up on MAN)*
Whimsically deranged by you,
I have now discovered,
you are, however easily I confuse,
you are disabled, too,
content to have withdrawn surrender.

WOMAN: No—no—no—not content,

(hearing his words as her own thoughts)

the word is not content at all—the word content
    is crippling now,
just as it crippled you before.

MAN: Then tell me, tell me…why—just whimsically?
    regard me, briefly, one final moment?

WOMAN: I do regard, and anything but briefly, you,
    who claim my blame for whimsical derangement,
    I feel, right now, and think, and act, just as I
    always have with you –

MAN: You –? Feel?

WOMAN: Yes –

MAN: Think?

WOMAN: Yes –

MAN: Act with me as always?

WOMAN: Yes, yes, I do…

MAN: Then this explains what seemed
    simply…unexplainable –

WOMAN: …I do…

MAN: …but hardly why you spend the time you've
    measured out in trying to write these words to
    me.

WOMAN: I know, I know, and yet, if only…
    If only you could have known me,
    now and then and when it mattered…

TOGETHER: Oh, yes…if…

MAN: …and if—and if—and if
    instead of if, forever if,
    'I do' had come from you…

TOGETHER: Oh, yes, I do –

WOMAN: I do….

> *(Long pause—then laughter from hysteria. Then complete change of tone.)*

Oh, yes, I do,
I need a mirror, I really do….

> *(More laughter, this time lighter, joined by MAN, then…)*

SECOND WOMAN: *(as older woman, neither visible yet.)* She needs a mirror….

MAN: And who are you?

WOMAN: A mirror in these rooms as big as me,
and here I'll sit pretending,
looking through this mirror, big as me and bigger,
pretending that I sit here, looking through this
mirror in my rooms,
pretending who I am. *(laughs)*

SECOND WOMAN: I am who I am and all of you…

MAN: You are? But….

WOMAN: …but proper pretense is exhausting –
Mirror, help me, for what I am I do and will –
but—who am I? *(brushes her hair humming)*

SECOND WOMAN: You see?

MAN: Oh, yes….Oh, no –

WOMAN: Am I so beautiful as I still seem to be?

SECOND WOMAN: You see? And who is she to you
unless you think of me,
of us?

MAN: Oh, no....

WOMAN: That's odd, now why should that occur to
me?

(both women—sustained laughter)

MAN: *(Now fully visible in forestage area, speaks over
laughter as it dies away)*
No, no, no, you can't go on and on and on –

(lights down slow halfway on WOMAN)

Can't you remember me a part of you?
Yet I must listen to you listening to yourself
commune with you,
within one there is no place for two, *(fading off)*

So...perhaps it's done and I shall simply
wait, and wait...and wait.
And discover...waiting, that while there is
still life,
there is this grand mystery. *(Lights up on
SECOND WOMAN)*

SECOND WOMAN: No place for two?

MAN: I think I understand some simple things.

SECOND WOMAN: And what—are simple things?

MAN: A smile, a shadow,
　　　a subtle flinching inward,
　　　a curiously misshapen circle,
　　　an unused line,
　　　a long-mistaken face –
　　　These things I think I understand.

SECOND WOMAN: And do you finally understand the
　　　cold?

MAN: The cold?

SECOND WOMAN: The dark beyond the harbor lights?

MAN: I'm not—sure.

SECOND WOMAN: You're not sure. As if such moments
　　　in the dark can drop so easily through grasping
　　　fingers and,
　　　as molten colored glass, be blown into the folly
　　　of an endless summer.

MAN: An endless summer? How was I to know the
　　　truth?

SECOND WOMAN: The truth? The truth was
　　　happening –

MAN: Oh my, oh my, oh my, and here instead of sealing
　　　love,
　　　a kiss has strangled you.

SECOND WOMAN: A kiss….oh what a chaste moon
　　　shown down that night….

MAN: You don't remember how I held you—how I
   loved you?
   I still love you.

SECOND WOMAN: You still love—but she is something
   else again,
   sitting there in mirrored judgment,
   aborting joy, dissolving grief
   in endless antithetical illusions....

MAN: No, not illusions, not just illusion –

SECOND WOMAN: What then? And what of us?
   You say that still you love –

WOMAN: They say that we're in love.
   To wit, to hold, they'd love to know
   the imagery we're in, they say.
   But just the other day –

MAN: And why should I lie breathless,
   encased in flesh unknown to me?

WOMAN: I know, I know…

MAN: It's true –

WOMAN: I know and still I say –

MAN: A moment ripens as it grows –

WOMAN: And still I say that you and I are quite in love –

MAN: …and while swinging quite unsteadily from
   one small branch –

WOMAN: Yes, quite in love –

MAN: …awaits its fall.

WOMAN: and now they say we've fallen, being in love,
    Oh yes, they say, we have,
    and having fallen, we are, so they pray,
    Now forever quite in love.

MAN: *(burying his face in his hands)*
    Now again the cavern,
    and always deep within the black,
    beyond the sound of water dripping,
    beyond the sound of human voices,
    a somber bell that's ringing….

WOMAN: Then let me say –

MAN: Yes, having fallen prey –

SECOND WOMAN: I pray we are forever –

WOMAN: Just in love –

MAN: For now –

WOMAN: For now –

MAN: Yes –

SECOND WOMAN: Having fallen –

WOMAN: – All the world is prey.

MAN: For to prey is not the same as play –

SECOND WOMAN: But…to play is to have fallen prey.

WOMAN: *(burst of wild laughter)*
    And everything is brilliantly so beautiful,
    Yes, I know, reflections cast reflections…

But *(fearfully)*....my own hand gone?
A premonition growing here in my own rooms,
in my own mirror?
I—I—faceless?

SECOND WOMAN: Such pretty sounds...such endless
shapes and symbols...
what varied playthings...*(laughs lightly),* you can't
count the number...

MAN: *(to SECOND WOMAN)*
Yes, it's toward you I'm slipping....down,
and with such unaccustomed pageantry –

SECOND WOMAN: You say that you still love me –

MAN: And if I choose, I can remember why,
and consequently lose my hold
on everything that's happening.

SECOND WOMAN: And still you say –

MAN: All right, all RIGHT—I choose this way –
My life is still my own, my structure, my design –

SECOND WOMAN: And what is she without the
imagery you taught her to believe in? The poetry
of feeling? The beauty of desire?

MAN: And what are you if I stop now?

SECOND WOMAN: You can't stop now.

MAN: That's right, but not because of what I am –
Because, then, you would cease to be
And this in turn would make a travesty

of everything I've ever done
and seen and felt and been a part of –
Without you, there would be little room
left for deceit, for lies and jealousy and envy –
My anger at myself would soon be voided,
pointless, a mimicry of my youth, of dreams –

SECOND WOMAN: But you have chosen to
remember....

MAN: Yes, I have, and I recall exactly what you said –

SECOND WOMAN: Not what was felt?

MAN: No, what was said that night you held me
on the waterfront –

(she weeps quietly)

You weep, but not for me –
We kissed and just before we kissed I said,
'I do not want to leave you'.

SECOND WOMAN: *(as YOUNG WOMAN, voice is
lighter, engaging)*
You don't have to leave,
stay here with me.
We'll go along to my flat,
I'll make you a delicious breakfast in the
morning.

MAN: Just tell me this is real, right now.
I must know something definite.
Sometimes I think...I want –

SECOND WOMAN: Then reach out…and reach again–

MAN: And how can you ask that?
How can you ask anything at all?
I remember you, but just remembering doesn't
change,
it doesn't ask or weep or anything.
I simply choose to not remember
and you cease to be at all.
You said that, still, you love me…
And still you cling, inexorably back down you
pull me.
Why?

SECOND WOMAN: Please….

*(long pause—when she speaks it is as his
mother)*

Please come down, you climb too high…

MAN: No, mother, when I fall
I want to plunge, not crawl from limb to limb –
If I can't soar wingless into some kind of
unknown victory,
I want to come down plunging, uncontrolled,
and smash the earth to pieces.

SECOND WOMAN: You, so small,
I can't hold you quite as easily as I once did, but
still you nestle in my arms and cling so
stubbornly to me.
My flesh, so quick,

Your hands, already large and grasping, hold my
     fingers, hold my hands,
as if some strange inheritance were ours to share,
Were ours within which we transcend together –
I feel as if within this moment,
     love gave meaning –
Wordless now, I give you mine.
I love you....

MAN: *(recalling his high school steady girl friend)*
And with your hand, once clenched in mine,
released,
you run swiftly on ahead, pause, and turn,
and then disappear.
A worried smile is all I have to think about till
     noon, when we will walk again together,
pressing shoulders secretly in teeming halls –
with twenty seven precious minutes ours to
     squander.

SECOND WOMAN:

*(lightly, her voice takes on that of his teen-aged
friend)*

Tomorrow, I will wear your favorite sweater,
And on Thursday, don't be moody,
we have so little time.

4. REINTEGRATION

WOMAN: *(cutting through, initiates cadenza which runs to end of scene)*
Dark –

SECOND WOMAN: We'll make some plans about the weekend –
Friday's out, of course,
but Saturday is ours.

WOMAN: Drop –

SECOND WOMAN: Please don't be late—Your hands are big, I love your hands

WOMAN: Blown –

SECOND WOMAN: When you are famous, may I hold your hand?
Will you remember me?
I'll always love you….

WOMAN: Chaste moon –

MAN: I was late on Saturday and ever after
late on every day –

SECOND WOMAN: *(in her original voice)* Dark –

MAN: And found, eventually, that lateness –

SECOND WOMAN: Drop –

MAN: Which I understand now as an aging process,

SECOND WOMAN: Blown –

MAN: Formed no escape, but left a dull and vaguely
   subtle sense of being ripened –

SECOND WOMAN: Chaste –

WOMAN: Bleak –

MAN: And I longed to climb a tree again.

SECOND WOMAN: Moon –

WOMAN: Autumnal tomb

MAN: Summer *is* forever.

SECOND WOMAN: Bleak autumnal tomb –

WOMAN: Chasing –

SECOND WOMAN: Chasing broken scarlet –

MAN: Chasing –

WOMAN: Broken scarlet shadows –

SECOND WOMAN: Shadows –

MAN: Broken shadows –

WOMAN: Gazing –

MAN: Chasing broken –

SECOND WOMAN: Gazing –

MAN: Scarlet shadows –

WOMAN & SECOND WOMAN: *(together)* Gazing –

MAN: Gazing –

WOMAN, MAN & SECOND WOMAN: *(together)*
   Lifelessly....

5. LEGACY

(Cross fade to YOUNG MAN and YOUNG WOMAN passionately entwined on a park bench at the edge of the waterfront. A little time passes. He rises from the bench.)

YOUNG MAN: It's cold. I'm cold.

YOUNG WOMAN: I've lived here all my life.
These streets—the buildings—this park—the waterfront...
you see the ocean just beyond the harbor lights?

YOUNG MAN: Beyond the harbor lights...*(looks back at her–returns to the bench)* I don't want to leave you.

(They kiss lovingly.)

YOUNG WOMAN: You don't have to leave –
stay here with me.
I'll make you a delicious breakfast in the morning.

YOUNG MAN: You don't understand,
I don't ever want to leave you...

YOUNG WOMAN: Ever is so long a time—things happen no one understands....
Be happy for a summer night –

YOUNG MAN: This summer is forever... *(shakes her head negatively)*

(He kisses her.)

Why let me kiss you then?

YOUNG WOMAN: You can't build forever on one kiss.

YOUNG MAN: Two, then – *(they kiss)*

YOUNG WOMAN: No, not even two.

YOUNG MAN: I don't understand you. Don't you feel anything?

(She draws him closer in answer.)

But… *(withdrawing)* I must talk.

YOUNG WOMAN: And talk it all away?

YOUNG MAN: Then it is different, not just another summer night, not just another moon, another guy?

(she studies him, they kiss)

Then talk to me.

YOUNG WOMAN: What shall I say?

YOUNG MAN: Tell me this is real, right now, and something great is happening.

YOUNG WOMAN: So this is how you have to have it happen?

YOUNG MAN: What? How do you mean?

YOUNG WOMAN: With poetry, the sound of words, the night, a kiss…

YOUNG MAN: I don't know. Sometimes I think—I want...

YOUNG WOMAN: Then reach out, and reach again...

YOUNG MAN: But you're the one...

YOUNG WOMAN: *(gently teasing)* Am I the one?

YOUNG MAN: Yes, you're the one that doesn't see, that won't believe...

YOUNG WOMAN: But I don't have to. This is enough for me tonight.

YOUNG MAN: What is enough?

YOUNG WOMAN: The happening, instead of dreaming.
There is no holding anything –

If that were true, you'd lose tonight as well, and, after all,
tonight I have much more than dreaming,
I have you...
Do you want me? *(kissing him tenderly)*

YOUNG MAN: I'm not sure now –
You make me feel as if tomorrow shouldn't matter,
and I can't help myself—it does.

(She pulls him to her, but he rises from the bench and moves away.)

It always has...as long as I remember.

There was mostly just tomorrows,
I still dream about it.

YOUNG WOMAN: ...dreaming dreams....
What kind of dream?

YOUNG MAN: *(slowly pacing back and forth)*
The same one—every time –
I walk along a street and somebody's beside me,
walking, hurrying on, together, not talking,
I just feel her there,
I don't know who she is...and then the corner –

I turn the corner, the wind whips at my coat, it's
cold. I put my collar up and keep walking faster
and I realize—I'm alone.

YOUNG WOMAN: Go on.

YOUNG MAN: And then I pass a door, an old carved,
oaken door, set so deeply in the city walls, I
almost miss it every time.

I stop, I can't help myself, and stare at it and,
finally, opening it slowly, I step inside into the
strange beauty of a quiet park at twilight.

The trees, the plants and shrubs all in bloom, the
velvet lawns—a little stream and on the stone
wall behind me, a small lamp flickering in the
gathering dusk—a graveled path unwinds away
from me into the undulating distance, into a
darkness. Compelled further into the scene, I

start down that winding path. Now and then, the lamp winks through the trees.

Finally, deep within the dusk, I hesitate, a shudder of fear passes through me.

YOUNG WOMAN: But why afraid?

YOUNG MAN: Afraid of what I see, I don't know why, still further on…

An old man, way on beyond where all the shadows run together, bending over, picking something up and slowly carrying it to put it somewhere in its place, as if the dark had places in it made for just that purpose. I start walking, faster this time, there—he's bending over, picking something up again, I can barely make him out, he's struggling this time, looking right toward me.

I call out to him, he's turning away… Wait… WAIT…

It doesn't matter, he's disappearing…I want to run but there's no path anywhere at all, I feel as if I'm choking and I want to scream out—to the old man—to anyone—and I try to scream but there's no air, I can't breathe. I know I must be dying but there isn't anything and there should be…something.

I'm all alone.

(*The YOUNG WOMAN, standing quietly, observing him, now helps him back to the bench. He sinks down with her, wrapping his arms around her, like a small boy would his mother.)*

Why must I dream that again?
What's wrong with me?
And what's not right enough?
You see, I really need tomorrow...I...this doesn't
     mean that time is running out.... for me?

YOUNG WOMAN: You have tonight,
     We have each other,
     Sleep a little bit...

(She speaks crooningly to him, he dozes off.)

Oh what a face....

(tracing his lips and nose and brows with one finger)

Your lips are tense,
Your body, sleeping, stiff and chilled.
You are so young and running,
Running after someone who'll say
     'follow me and love',
But love is running then as well...
Our love is here...

I love you.

6. Chorus of Fears

(Slow fade for cross to Park interior, lights dim, a group of children come running into the park, their faces painted black or white with fine vertical striping, calling softly to each other.)

CHILDREN....Reenan? Hey, Ronan, over here...Riddlekin...Rennelman...Let's go, let's go...Rankin.... Hey, Runkin—where you been? There's Ripran, over there.... Rudroff...Come on, Rottlemyer, come ON!

(Although they feint and play with each other as they gather, there seems to be no indecision about their role and consequent action. It should become obvious that they have done this many times before, as a ritual of their own. Finally, circling around the sleeping couple they begin their dance chorus. The mood is grotesque, macabre.)

Hey—Hey—Hey—Hey—*(laughter)*
Run, run, run around,
up and out and down and through,
Now you have just four more times
to guess exactly—Who are you? *(Bell)*
A lover? A lover? A lover? A lover?
NOOOOOOOOOO No No No No

Guess again, guess again, guess again, guess again,
Now you know, now you don't,
Now you can, now you won't!

(More laughter—while they dance, they play a word game.)

INDIVIDUAL VOICES: Closure!
Closure –
Closure what?
Closure eyes? *(laughter)*
Veeeeeeeerrrrge constricting!
Beautiful –
You're beautiful!
I AM DESIRE!
I'm not –
Why not?

TOGETHER: *My Act Is Set!*
Wheeeeeeeeeee!
Deranged –
Desire –
Forgotten –
Youth –
Proof?
(chanted)
Dawn!
Death!
Truth!

(They clap as if applauding but do so in rhythm.)

Hey—Hey—Hey—Hey—*(laughter)*
Run, run, run around, *(circling couple again)*
Up and out and down and through,
Now you have just three more times
to guess exactly—Who are you? *(bell)*
A thief? A thief? A thief? A thief?
NOOOOOOOOOO No No No No
Guess again—guess again—guess again—guess
     again,
Now you know, Now you don't,
Now you can, Now you won't!

(more laughter as they continue word game)

INDIVIDUAL VOICES: Chaste!
     Chaste –
     Chaste taste?
     Chaste waste! *(laughter)*
     Dark –
     Drop –
     Blown –
     Tooooooooommmmmmb!
     I AM STARING!
     You're not caring!
     That's beautiful!
     That's me!

TOGETHER: Wheeeeeeeeeeeee!
     Deranged –
     Desire –

Forgotten –
Youth –

(chanted)

Proof?
Dawn!
Death!
Truth! *(clapping as before)*
Hey—Hey—Hey—Hey—*(laughter)*
Run, run, run around, *(circling couple again)*
up and out and down and through.
Now you have just two more times
to guess exactly—Who are you? *(bell)*
A saint? A saint? A saint? A saint?
Nooooooooooooooooooo No No No No
Guess again—guess again—guess again—guess
      again –
Now you know, now you don't,
now you can, now you won't—

(laughter, dance continues word game)

INDIVIDUAL VOICES: Mirror!
      Mirror who?
      Mirror me –
      Mirror do! *(laughter)*
      Cotton –
      Candy –
      Get's all –
      Sandy!

I'm still handy!
You're desire –
You're waiting –
WE ARE WAITING!
Lifelessly –
......Lifelessly –
............Lifelessly –
That's beautiful!
That's me!

TOGETHER: Wheeeeeeeeeeeeeeeeee!
Deranged –
Desire –
Forgotten –
Youth –

(chanted)

Proof?
Dawn!
Death!
Truth! *(clapping as before, wild shrieks of laughter)*
Hey—Hey—Hey—Hey—
Run, run, run around,
Up and down and out and through,
Now you have just one more time,
to guess exactly—Who are you? *(bell)*

(Within their midst, dancers discover one of themselves to be an old man.)

An old man?
An old man!
ooooooooooooooooh yeeeeeeeeeeeees,

(quietly, knowingly)

An old man….

7. TREE HOUSE

(Exit calling softly to each other with slow fade to Night, young boy in his tree house, several children on ground beneath tree)

YOUNG BOY: No, you don't.

CHILDREN: Yes, we do. Oh yes, we do –

BOY: No, you don't, you can't…

CHILDREN: We know a secret *(laughing)*

BOY: Go on, go on, you don't have to be here anyway –

CHILDREN: Yes, we do, yes, we do, we know a secret –

  (more laughter, fading)

BOY: A secret…*(to himself)*, I don't have a secret – What's the matter with them anyway?

  (heard from other side of garden wall)

SECOND WOMAN: Please come down, you climb so high, I can hardly see you in the moonlight…

BOY: Oh, mother…No—I won't! I will not! *(pause)* She doesn't understand…I can't!

CHILDREN: He will not, he cannot, *(taunting)* not now, in the moonlight –
That's his secret, that's his secret, that's his awful secret.

BOY: Stop it! That's not true –

FIRST CHILD: Then come down –

SECOND CHILD : Yes, then come down and play
    with us!

BOY: I *am* playing with you.

THIRD: Oh, come on…

FOURTH You think you are…

BOY: I am.

FIFTH: But you're not—because you can't!

SIXTH: Not really!

BOY: I am, I am, who says I'm not? You don't know what
    I can see up here –

SECOND WOMAN: Be careful—Please, be careful, you
    might hurt yourself. I used to play with you, I
    used to hold you in my arms. Are you all right?
    I can hardly see you in the moonlight.

BOY: I'm all right, I'm just here, resting for a minute.

CHILDREN: *(laughing softly)* Worry, worry, worry, worry.

BOY: Stop it! Stop it! Leave her out of this, she'll be all
    right, she'll change, you'll see….

FIRST CHILD: If she can worry…

SECOND: Like she does…

THIRD: Like she always will…

YOUNG BOY: She can't help it –

FOURTH: Yes, she can – *(snatching cap away)*

SECOND: Hey! Give that back! *(They toss cap around in keepaway game.)*

THIRD: It's mine, it's mine!

FIFTH: It belongs to everybody –

THIRD: Well, it's mine now –

SIXTH: No, it isn't, and you know it!

SECOND: That's right, so give it back to me –

> *(Children continue to squabble in background.)*

BOY: You don't understand, that's all *(to himself)*, she can't help herself, she can't help…right now. Perhaps tomorrow…

SECOND WOMAN: *(gently imitating voice of GIRL)* Tomorrow I will wear your favorite sweater –

BOY: Or the next day –

SECOND WOMAN: And on Thursday, don't be moody.

BOY: Or the next –

SECOND WOMAN: Friday's out, of course –

BOY: There's time, there really is so much time –

SECOND WOMAN: Yes, Saturday's ours—please don't be late –

BOY: *(angrily)* Well, can't *you* wait?

SECOND WOMAN: *(lower, harshly)* I'll wait!

CHILDREN: Hating waiting, wanting waiting,
   That's his secret, that's his awful secret –

BOY: It is not! That's not true, it isn't true...

   (children laughing lightly)

   Leave me alone, just leave me alone....*(to himself)*
   I can't stay here....

8. Cross Dimensions

SECOND WOMAN: *(imitating voice of young woman)*
    Why not?
    I've lived here all my life,
    this garden, these quaint streets,
    these buildings, this little park –
    The waterfront –
    Can you see the ocean from up there,
    just beyond the harbor lights?

BOY: I'm cold—I can't stay here –

SECOND WOMAN: You're young and already running after someone who might say. 'Follow me, come follow me…..'

BOY: Not me,

CHILDREN: Run, run, run around up and down and out and through –

BOY: Not me,

SECOND WOMAN: *(in voice of mother)*
    Please come down.

BOY: I want to climb, that's all –

SECOND WOMAN: You'll fall –

BOY: All right, ALL RIGHT! Yes, I might,

    (His voice grow clear, unexpectedly strong.)

    But when I fall,

I want to PLUNGE, not crawl
from limb to limb,
Always hanging, holding on,

(Children back off alarmed and exit quietly.)

If I can't soar wingless into some kind of
          unknown victory,
I'd rather come down plunging, uncontrolled,

(quietly)

and smash the earth to pieces –

(distantly as fadeout begins)

and smash the earth to pieces....

9. And You Are…?

(Continue cross fade to a beach, a small park, one or two benches. The children wander in like a small group of homeless kids.)

MAN: *(pacing slowly near a bench, reading out loud from book he is holding)*
"…two casual forms, their youth a beautiful
      facade,
As if a spray-laced seaweed fan held trembling
could conceal the heart we hide,
For beauty, like the pulse, cannot be clutched,
cannot be kept in place,

(BOY and GIRL are dimly seen together on the water's edge)

Those castled sands whose dense particled
collage, once moistened, toes hopelessly attempt
to hold together,
Sands lingering, withdrawing, free.
Each tide drift pulls away, relieves, destroys,
      non-entity….

FIRST CHILD *(appears unnoticed by the MAN)*
What are you doing?

MAN: *(startled)* I'm….reading a poem –

SECOND CHILD: Out loud?

(children gather around)

MAN: Well, yes....

THIRD CHILD: What a funny thing to be doing –

(laughter)

MAN: You might say, I was unaware of my audience –

FOURTH CHILD: What's he mean?

FIFTH CHILD: I don't know!

SIXTH CHILD: He must be crazy! *(more laughter)*

FIRST CHILD: Play with us Mr. Poem –

SECOND CHILD: Yes, yes, play with us –

MAN: All right, all right, but what shall we play?

THIRD CHILD: Blind Man's Bluff!

FOURTH CHILD: I know, Simon Says!

MAN: All right, Simon Says.

FIFTH CHILD: Wait! Wait! Simon must be an old man!

SIXTH CHILD: Are you an old man?

MAN: Well, not exactly, at least –

FIRST CHILD: That's all right, we'll make you old!

> *(Laughter; they scurry off to come back with an old blanket, scarf, driftwood cane, dressing him up, then standing back to inspect him.)*

SECOND CHILD: Much better, much better –

THIRD CHILD: Now he really is an old man –

MAN: Now listen! Simon Says—Run around! *(children run in circles)*
Sit on the ground! *(voices fading)*

10. ON THE BEACH

(Cross fade to pick up GIRL: sitting with BOY: by the beach.)

GIRL: You're very naughty –

BOY: Why?

GIRL: You know very well—we should be in class right
   now.
   What a thought—I can hear her now *(imitating
      teacher)*
   'Reenan, Ronan, Riddlekin, Rankin, Runkin—
      Hurry along,
   please—you are late—get out your cards
      quickly—I have
   some questions for today….Rankin? Absent.
      Runkin…?
   Absent? Hmmnn, both absent, again!' *(both
      laughing lightly, amused)*
   Hi, Rankin….

BOY: *(affectionately)* Hello….Runkin –

   (slight self-conscious pause)

GIRL: But we should go back soon –

BOY: Why? What for?

GIRL: ….just a feeling, before it's too late –

BOY: Too late? Hah! I'm never going back—I'm sick of pretending and all the rest…

GIRL: What are you going to do then? What else is there to do?

BOY: Plenty! *(uncertainly)* There's plenty to do, I'm just not sure about what right now, that's all.…

(She puts her hand over his, in a brief spontaneous gesture, but he withdraws).

CHILDREN: Simon Says—Tell me a story.
Yes, yes, you must!
Simon *must* tell a story!

(MAN has gotten up from park bench and appears to be preoccupied with the two figures by the beach—but then allows himself to be pulled to the ground by the children where he makes himself comfortable in their midst.)

MAN: Once upon a time, long ago.…

FIRST CHILD: How long ago?

MAN: As long ago as you can imagine –

SECOND CHILD: Were you there?

MAN: Where?

THIRD CHILD: A long time ago?

MAN: Yes, *(chuckling)* yes, I was there…

FOURTH CHILD: Go on, go on…

MAN: In a strange and mysterious castle, I discovered
that a beautiful princess—oh yes, very beautiful,
was locked, all by herself, in a tower...

FIFTH CHILD: Why?

MAN: No one could tell me why –

*(Children start singing lightly in the back-
ground.)*

CHILDREN: Run, run run around –
Up and out and
down and through,
now you have just four more times,
to guess exactly –
Who are you? *(Bell. Children's voices fade away.)*
A lover? A lover? A lover? A lover?

11. SAND CASTLE

(Lights up bright on BOY and GIRL—abrupt change of mood)

GIRL: I'm BORED!

BOY: My Lady?

GIRL: Yes?

BOY: Allow me—an entertainment!

GIRL: Well?

BOY: First, some finishing touches on this castle...*(sculpting pretend castle)*

GIRL: What for? What's the castle for?

BOY: For you.

GIRL: Me?

BOY: Yes. You will be my bored Lady of the Castle Built of Sand.

GIRL: Impossible!

BOY: Perhaps, but impossibly so, nevertheless.

GIRL: *(sighs, to herself)* I'm afraid—no one can be someone else's anything....

BOY: AHA! *(she jumps)* You see? In my castle, there are no doors, just windows!

GIRL: *Must* you play games?

BOY: I only meant, I shall pretend there are no doors....

GIRL: But that's what I mean....

BOY: All right then, we shall have doors, but without handles –

GIRL: *Why* must you pretend?

BOY: Why not?

GIRL: *(resuming earlier, youthful voice)* You make things seem, well, creepy!

BOY: It's a 'creepy' castle, with long 'creepy' corridors, and at night, the wind sighs down the corridors. And the doors –

GIRL: – the 'pretend doors without handles'?

BOY: The doors bang now and then, creaking on their rusty hinges –

GIRL: *That's* creepy –

BOY: *(softly)* And the doors without handles bang in the wind on their rusty hinges –

GIRL: My toes are getting wet....*(pulling her feet further up under her)*

BOY: *(distracted)*And down the lonely corridors, the wind sighs.... yes.... And it's so dark—you can't see your hand....

GIRL: Let's turn on some lights –

BOY: Ah! There *are* no lights—just sounds –

GIRL: No people?

BOY: No one! Just sounds and feelings….and the wind sighing –

GIRL: Where am I?

BOY: Why—you're in the tower, in your rooms—at the other end of the castle –

GIRL: What am I doing there?

BOY: You're waiting.

GIRL: Waiting?

BOY: Waiting. *(distant sound of wind)*
Waiting for your lover.

GIRL: Who?

BOY: Me.

GIRL: Oh. Then what?

BOY: See, down below, in the garden all lit with candles…

(Sounds of laughter, occasional lines are heard: "Oh what a lovely night" and "Champagne anyone?" BOY and GIRL are looking down into the "garden" fascinated.)

…the guests have arrived, they've started without you! They're drinking champagne! *(he turns toward her)*

GIRL: *(continues looking, absorbed in what she sees)*

BOY: They're laughing! They're…..dancing!

GIRL: *(there is a sudden sharp knock on the door)*
Who was….what was that?

(distant sound of glasses breaking)

BOY: They've drunk a toast to you, don't be afraid—
Open the door.

GIRL: *(a little breathless)*…I can't!

BOY: *I'll* open it.

GIRL: It's you!

BOY: It's me! But you—you are so beautiful tonight,
such a lovely gown –

*(Her hands move to her body, as if smoothing
down her gown, at the same time she shrinks
away from him.)*

Don't be afraid, you *must* come, here—
take my hand –

(light down to dim)

GIRL: It's so dark, I…hear your breathing….

*(Sounds from the party rise, then subside and
fade out.)*

BOY: We're almost there –

*(Pacing accelerates as if injected with nervous
energy to close of scene.)*

GIRL: I know—watch out for the steps –

I....can't see anything—*(highly alarmed)*
What's happened to the candles?

BOY: *(intense, excited, low pitched)*

It's too late! The people are leaving, the sea has broken through the wall and the garden is filling with water!

Quickly, there is no time to lose—your gown—it's getting wet!

(swooping her up in his arms)

MAN: *(in darkness, excitedly)* "....he picks her up and starts to
walk down the steps into the water.
It is black and warm, little waves come swirling around
his knees...."

GIRL: *(suddenly struggling furiously)* Let *go!* LET GO!

(BOY loses his balance, they tumble down together and lock in passionate embrace—finding each other's lips frantically—they kiss—then she breaks away violently.)

I'm leaving, I'm sick of this....pretending –

BOY: Wait, don't go—

(GIRL rises, brushes off sand, fixes hair.)

I'm not finished –

GIRL: It's a horrible story—I feel like crying.
Why must you pretend? Why?

BOY: But—I'm not pretending!

(GIRL walks away, faint light on MAN and one child.)

...I'm *not* pretending –

(BOY fades out.)

MAN: *(as GIRL: exits past MAN, he reaches out to her in gesture of an old man)*
Wait...Wait...
There was nothing meant by that –
Can't you see, he *loves* you....*(GIRL: exits)*

(CHILD hiding behind MAN, peers around and calls after GIRL: in stage whisper while MAN: holds arm out in frozen gesture)

CHILD *Simon* says 'he *loves* you'....

12. DESIRE

(Cross fade to DINNER PARTY, spot picks up YOUNG BOY, who witnesses the following from perch in tree near garden wall. MAN, as originally seen, is pouring champagne for everyone.)

YOUNG MAN/YOUNG WOMAN: Thank you! Thank you very much!

YOUNG WOMAN: I say, isn't all this –

MAN: —simply beautiful!

SECOND WOMAN: To wit!

MAN: A toast?

GIRL: To wit, to woo, to win!

(All drink, sound of harpsichord music, MAN lively chatter, YOUNG BOY is dimly visible in tree.)

SECOND WOMAN: *(moving to sideboard buffet)* How devastating! Oysters!

YOUNG WOMAN: And no R in the month!

GIRL: Of course, darling, and all the more enchanting!

SECOND WOMAN: *(laughter—music—talk)* Champagne, champagne, and more champagne!

YOUNG MAN: *(pouring SECOND WOMAN's glass)*

MAN: Is green deeper than blue?

>*(pouring YOUNG WOMAN's glass)*

Can love be wise?

>*(pouring GIRL's glass)*

Are you in lieu! *(much laughter)*
To wit, to woo, to win!

WOMEN: A toast! A toast!

MEN: We have a toast!

GIRL: *(raising glasses)* To –? *(silence)*

ALL To Desire....long live Desire—*(silence—they drink—then more laughter)*

BOY: Very good, very good, indeed, excellent, in fact!

ALL: *(music, more laughter)*
Would you dance?

YOUNG MAN: *(in response)* Oh yes, that is, I do!

SECOND WOMAN: I would! that is to say –

GIRL: We dance divinely—when we would....would you?

YOUNG MAN: Yes!

>*(The three women and the YOUNG MAN join hands and the four of them swirl to the waltz music, strings added.)*

ALL: Yes! Yes!

(A litter, carried by four or more students, is brought in carrying the WOMAN wearing a death mask. It is placed in center as if it was a banquet table. Litter should be sloped forward so that WOMAN can be seen full length by audience. Everyone notices her lifeless form only casually. Otherwise, dancing continues, chatter continues, laughter rises and subsides.)

BOY: Ah, yes! At last!

(All give pleasant attention to the litter.)

SECOND WOMAN: Desire is here.

YOUNG MAN: Here, with us? *(noticing litter for first time)* How fitting and how....nice!

MAN: Oh, yes indeed! But—let us consider:
to eat, and to sleep, and to love under glass,
is not as pleasant for the pheasant!

(everyone nods knowingly)

SECOND WOMAN: Can love be wise?

GIRL: She is so beautiful.

YOUNG MAN: And so are you! Your gown is exquisite!

BOY: And you smell delicious!

ALL: Oh, what a lovely evening!

MAN: And she *(nodding toward litter)* is very fond of it, as well.

YOUNG WOMAN: What thoughts!

YOUNG MAN: What feelings!

GIRL: But such imagery – how strange!

MAN: She knows—she knows—I really think she knows!

SECOND WOMAN: Impossible!

ALL: Impossible?

YOUNG WOMAN: This *is* summer....

YOUNG MAN: And summer is forever –

GIRL: How terribly pleasant, really, and how nice....

> *(Pall bearers move in and slowly walk out with litter.)*

BOY: Oh? Must she go so soon? *(they exit)* I suppose so.

MAN: I wonder, though, I wonder who she really is?

SECOND WOMAN: *(lowering voice)* Did you feel that?

BOY: Can't you feel that?

YOUNG WOMAN: Yes...I believe I can...

MAN: Yes...*I* can, I *think* I can.... No....
I *do*! I *do* feel that?

SECOND WOMAN: I thought as much.

MAN: You did?

GIRL: Yes...no....she did.

YOUNG WOMAN: Oh yes, and what a lovely night...

ALL: Oh, what a lovely night.

MAN: Champagne, anyone?

ALL: Champagne? Yes, yes, champagne and more
champagne!

(music, laughter, dancing resumes)

MAN: Well then, shall we drink…to dawn?

(raising glass)

ALL: To death? To truth? No, no, no, no, never!

MAN: To what then?

ALL: To Desire!

*(Glasses clink, laughter, scene slowly dissolves
until only MAN, downstage, and YOUNG
BOY, in tree, are dimly visible.)*

MAN: *(chuckling to himself)* That's good, that's really
good! *(he drinks)*
That's very good, indeed!

*(Slow fade to blackout. Half lights up slowly,
desks are arranged in different directions.
Young men/young women are seated at each
and talking among each other. The Leader
tends toward the severe, to the point, humor-
less. Students put up with her but underneath
they are a little fearful.)*

13. CLASSROOM

LEADER: Order, more order...
Reenan? Ronan? Riddlekin? Rankin? Runkin? –

Hurry along, please—You are late—Get your
cards out quickly, I have some questions for today.
Rankin? Absent?
Runkin...Absent? Hmm, both absent...again!
Ripran? Rudroff? Rottlemeyer? Good.
Let us pick up the thread.
Let us continue our creating.
Use your cards.
This is a seminar.
Most important to think.
Even more important to contribute right
answers.
Rennelman, sit up! Riddlekin—What makes
invalid an historical continuum?

RIDDLEKIN: Just equilibrium.

LEADER: Good. Wrong. Not right enough, that is. For
example—Where are we today, Reenan?

REENAN: Where we were yesterday.

LEADER: Right. Fair. Not wrong enough, that is. Can we
say, we have, at any rate, not moved ahead?
Ripran?

RIPRAN: Moving ahead is a concept.

LEADER: Well, apparently that is to be considered.

RIPRAN: Falling behind is a concept.

LEADER: Yes, that as well.

RIPRAN: Immobility is a concept.

RONAN: Ripran has three concepts right there.

RENNELMAN: Three makes a circle.

RUDROFF: A circle is in equilibrium.

ROTTLEMEYER: No continuum.

UNISON: Historically!

LEADER: Excellent! You excite me!
    Sit up, Rottlemeyer –
    Where are we?

REENAN: We are past the verge of closure.

RONAN: Reenan's right.

REENAN: So is Ronan.

RIDDLEKIN: Reenan and Ronan are word weavers.

REENAN/RONAN: Thank you, thank you—all of you.
    Thank you very much indeed. Thank –

LEADER: Sit Down Immediately!
    That's better.
    This is a seminar.
    Stick to your answer cards or I am forced to erase
        your names.
    Sit up, Rudroff! Rennelman?

RENNELMAN: We have some space –

RIPRAN: …since Rankin and Runkin have already been erased.

RONAN: Ripran's right.

REENAN: So is Rennelman.

RUDROFF: Since we have space, we have their time as well.

ROTTLEMEYER: And consequently silence.

LEADER: Silence?

UNISON: Silence…

LEADER: Silence!

RIPRAN: Silence, space and time outline desire.

LEADER: *Let Me!*
As long as we are here, let us proceed.
Exactly.
Let us not get too involved.
Rather, let us talk, instead, about what's
happened.

UNISON: Let us talk about what's happened.

LEADER: What we think about what's happened.

UNISON: What we think about what's happened.

LEADER: What we feel for what we think has
happened.

UNISON: What we feel for what we think has
happened.

LEADER: And remember –

UNISON: And remember –

LEADER: ...to remember –

UNISON: ...to remember –

LEADER: ...what we feel of what we think about what's happened –

UNISON: ...yes...yes...yeeeees...

LEADER: ...is to know her reality!

UNISON: Yea————————————!

LEADER: Stop It! Stooooooooop It!
No demonstrations! Please! We can't afford them. This is a <u>seminar</u> about what is happening. May we begin?

RIPRAN: There is a woman.

RONAN: The woman is alone.

LEADER: Good, good.

RIDDLEKIN: She is finally alone with the man.

RENNELMAN: But—the man is alone.

LEADER: Right! Good! Wrong! Well?

RIPRAN: He is alone with a second woman.

LEADER: Aha! Go on, go on...

RUDROFF: She is alone.

ROTTLEMEYER: She is a mother.

REENAN: She is a girl.

RONAN: She is a young woman.

LEADER: Excellent! You see? I'm terribly excited…
    This—is the beginning!
    Please, continue!

RIDDLEKIN: Reenan and Ronan are right.

RENNELMAN: So is Riddlekin…

LEADER: Yes, yes, yes, yes, Rennelman,
    I know, I know, I know. But can't you
    consider the flow, the flow?

RIPRAN: There is a young man.

RUDROFF: He is alone.

ROTTLEMEYER: The young man is with a young
    woman.

UNISON: They are alone with each other.

LEADER: Yes, yes, yes, yes –

REENAN: The young man dreams a dream.

RONAN: The dream is happening.

RIDDLEKIN: Both Reenan and Ronan are right.

RENNELMAN: So is Riddlekin.

LEADER:

RENNELMAN: The young woman watches the young
    man's dream while it's happening.

RIPRAN: There is an old man in the dream.

RUDROFF: He has been alone for a long time.

ROTTLEMEYER: He is alone with some children.

REENAN: /RONAN: They have been alone for a short time.

OTHERS: Everyone is all together.

LEADER: Please!

RIDDLEKIN: But Reenan and Ronan are right, just the same.

OTHERS: So is Riddlekin!

LEADER: Please, please! Rennelman?

RENNELMAN: In the dream, the old man is putting everything in place.

RIPRAN: But he dies.

RUDROFF: It is very unfortunate for now there is nothing to put in place.

UNISON: There *is* no place to put *nothing*.

ROTTLEMEYER: But now is too late to happen anyway.

REENAN: Now is a closure.

RONAN: We are studying closures and what we feel about it when it happens, right?

RIDDLEKIN: Right!

RENNELMAN: Riddlekin is –

LEADER: *Never Mind!* No, no, not you! Yes! Go ahead…

RIPRAN: There are two students missing.

ROTTLEMEYER: They are in love.

RUDROFF: They are studying one another.

UNISON: They are very bad. They have been *erased*.

LEADER: Wait a minute…

REENAN: It is more important to study ends and
means.

RONAN: Soon we will study what their end means.

LEADER: Wait—just wait…

RIDDLEKIN: He is going to build a castle out of sand.

LEADER: Please, stop…

RENNELMAN: She is going to die in it.

LEADER: Can't you hear me?

UNISON: They are both going to –

LEADER: Wait—Go back—Quickly!

RENNELMAN: She is going to die in it.

TEACHER: Quickly—Faster-

RIDDLEKIN: He is going to build a castle out of sand.

LEADER: Faster! Run! Run!

UNISON: They are very bad.

ROTTLEMEYER: They are in love.

WOMAN: *They say that we're in love…*

LEADER: Please, RUN!

RONAN: We are studying closure.

REENAN: Now is a closure.

ROTTLEMEYER: But now is too late to happen, anyway.

LEADER: No! No, please—*stretch your breath* –

RIPRAN: There is an old man in the dream.

RONAN: The dream is happening.

WOMAN: *They would love to know the imagery we're in.*

LEADER: Runraced…Stretch your rushing breath!

ROTTLEMEYER: The young man is alone with a young woman.

RUDROFF: They are both –

UNISON: Alone.

LEADER: …face fastening hard…

WOMAN: If only you could have known me,
    Now and then and when it mattered…

LEADER: Breathe up through colored tiers –
    Through glass planes –
    This is the beginning.

RIDDLEKIN: She is finally alone with a man.

(Lighting starts down)

WOMAN: Yes, yes, but *where are you?*

LEADER: In space coagulating slowly – Ripran?

RIPRAN: When what there is in life that stifles,

suffocates and finally blocks all action –
forms no target…

*(Low spot picks up WOMAN: walking slowly
toward her original position in front of the
mirror.)*

RONAN: The woman is alone.

REENAN: There *is* a woman…

LEADER: …staring…

UNISON: A woman…staring…

LEADER: Motionless –

(complete cross fade to WOMAN)

14. Moment's End

(WOMAN resumes her original spot, seated in front of the mirror frame through which she views the audience.)

I think, perhaps,
there is no moment madness starts –
The moment, yes…
This moment, here—around me…
a calculated texture through which pass tangents
binding what is past with what is happening
right now,
and webbing me, strung taut, into the future.

Is this fear staring back from black?

Or you?

You say you've tried to reach me now
for many days – And yet I saw you yesterday,
and not content to speak,
you touched me.

Yes…I spoke to you and touched you back,
and watched your staring eyes
that would not leave the water…
Watched you etch a still life

on the surface of that pond
and despondently collect reflections.

You staring back from black—
Your breath, as on a pane of glass,
made mist across the water...
I think, perhaps, my truth, within these walls,
is only partially revealed,
a premonition grown in structured air,
arched lazily...and slowly swollen...
Brings pretense to a sharpened edge.

What happened to the castle made of sand?

This moment drifting through the afternoon,
While numbered flecks form stealthy spheres,
Rift welling...welling up through...
fleet...second growth.

(Start slow fade then go to blackout.)

– Finis –